WITHAM 'N' BLUES
IT ALL COMES OUT IN THE WASH

MIKE MURPHY

CRANTHORPE
—MILLNER—
PUBLISHERS

Copyright © Mike Murphy (2024)

The right of Mike Murphy to be identified as author of this work has been asserted by them in accordance with section 77 and 78 of the Copyright, Designs and Patents Act 1988.

All rights reserved. No part of this publication may be reproduced, stored in a retrieval system, or transmitted in any form or by any means, electronic, mechanical, photocopying, recording, or otherwise, without the prior permission of the publishers.

Any person who commits any unauthorised act in relation to this publication may be liable to criminal prosecution and civil claims for damages.

This book is a work of fiction. Names, characters, places and incidents are either products of the author's imagination or are used fictitiously.

First published by Cranthorpe Millner Publishers (2024)

ISBN 978-1-80378-195-2 (Paperback)

www.cranthorpemillner.com

Cranthorpe Millner Publishers

Printed and bound by CPI Group (UK) Ltd
Croydon, CR0 4YY

To my wife, Michele, for all her help and support

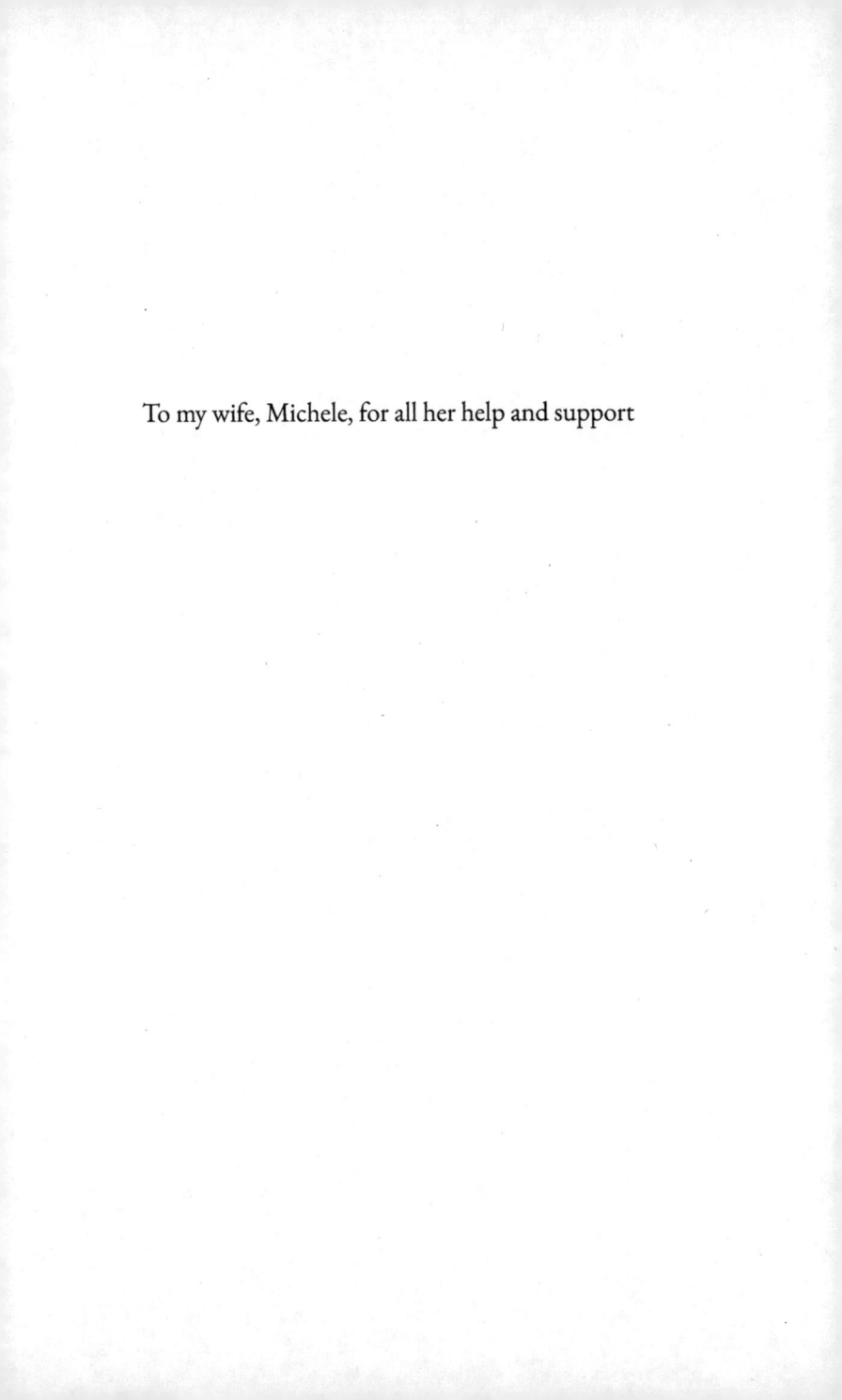

CONTENTS

CHAPTER 1   1
From Buttholeville, Alabama, to Lindum via Newark (Twice)

CHAPTER 2   8
The First Team Meeting: Down to Work

CHAPTER 3   14
Gainsborough – Sunday All Week Long

CHAPTER 4   30
A Most Unexpected Trip to London

CHAPTER 5   39
Boston: The Capital of Brassica and Cultural Mick's

CHAPTER 6   64
Brassica, the Vinyl Triangle and the Deep South

CHAPTER 7   79
Radio Brassica and Some Office Work

CHAPTER 8   88
On to Market Rasen and Horncastle

CHAPTER 9	95

  The Festivals They Could Not Stop!

CHAPTER 10	102

  Radio Free Brassica

CHAPTER 11	110

  Market Rasen (Again)

CHAPTER 12	118

  The Day Train to Cleethorpes and Grimsby

CHAPTER 13	127

  Louth, the Laurel Canyon of Lincs

CHAPTER 14	137

  Back to the Cabbage Studio, Washing and Bob's

CHAPTER 15	146

  Lincoln Yields Some of its Secrets

CHAPTER 16	153

  Taking (Vegetable) Stock

CHAPTER 17	159

  Woodhall Ska "This Town – Looking Like a Golf Town"

CHAPTER 18	170

  Sleaford: No Mods Here

CHAPTER 19	172

  Boston, Rap and Brat Pack

CHAPTER 20	180

  A Visit to Skegness and the Caravana Coast

CHAPTER 21	187

  Stamford Punk Central

CHAPTER 22	192

  Getting Ready for the Big Show and a Shock

CHAPTER 23	199
Missing the Boss	
CHAPTER 24	203
Rehearsal: Show Time Minus One	
CHAPTER 25	214
The Big Day (and Night)	
CHAPTER 26	232
The Happy Ever After Party?	
CHAPTER 27	241
After the Lord Mayor's Show... Back to Reality	
APPENDICES	i
ACKNOWLEDGEMENTS	ix
ABOUT THE AUTHOR	x

CHAPTER 1

From Buttholeville, Alabama, to Lindum via Newark (Twice)

Professor Otis Kevin "OK" Spanner III was exhausted. The extended nature of modern intercontinental travel made it feel like he had been in a state of suspended animation, and the same suit, for several days.

His journey had started from his office at the University of Toscahonee, Alabama, with a drive to Birmingham. Every time he visited Birmingham he recalled the words of the great Randy Newman, who claimed that Birmingham was, "The greatest city in Alabam."

Sheer poetry, thought Otis, *and sure hard to doubt.*

No time to enjoy its many delights today, however, as it was straight to the airport for a flight to Newark – New Jersey – and a connecting flight to London's Heathrow.

It was many hours later that the Piccadilly Line delivered him and his not inconsiderable luggage to King's Cross railway station, where he boarded a train going north.

He thought to himself, *that's the second time today this southern boy's going north.*

His instructions told him to stay on the train until Newark and then change trains for Lincoln. The train journey was pretty smooth, uneventful even, and Otis had become lulled into a light sleep when the door at the end of the carriage burst open and about twenty, liberally tattooed youths, charged through chanting:

'We are Leeds, we are Leeds, we are Leeds, we are Leeds, we are Leeds, we are Leeds, we are Leeds, we are Leeds, we are Leeds, *we are Leeds*!'

Everyone else in the carriage seemed to shrink down into their seats and stare pointedly out of the windows, as if the fields and hedgerows had suddenly become particularly interesting. The procession passed through the door at the far end of the carriage and a strange silence hung in the air.

Otis, by now rudely awake, turned to his fellow passenger and asked, 'What are "leeds"?'

She replied, 'That lot? Football fans. Welcome to England.'

On to Grantham which, even though on the main line, didn't look to have much about it. Then the next station, Newark, was announced.

Deja vu, thought Otis, hoping he hadn't been going round in circles.

At Newark he had to cross the passenger bridge to commence the final stage of his marathon excursion where, on platform three, the Lincoln train was waiting, belching diesel fumes into the atmosphere. As Otis crossed the bridge over the mainline, he had this feeling that he was moving into another dimension, a slower world, not unlike the South back home.

The Lincoln train, a short boxy single carriage, sat there vibrating, its windows caked in grime. Then his eyes caught the station sign "Newark Northgate" in large black letters. Underneath someone had added, "Twinned with purgatory". In another, cruder hand, some wit had written "Newark – anagram of wanker".

Oh dear, thought Otis and, with that thought fresh in his mind, the train beeped twice, juddered and, in a cloud of brown diesel fumes, set off for the final leg of his journey.

In truth, though the trip had been long in the planning, Otis didn't really know too much about the country he was now to reside in for the next year. He recalled reading a rare piece of foreign news in *The Huntsville Times*, or it could have been *The Buttholeville Bugle*, that the Brits had decided to pull out of some Eurovision contest in order to save £350 a week to spend on caring for old folks in hospitals. The article had a picture of a bus with £350 on its side. He couldn't remember why, though. He'd heard that train fares were expensive in the UK but, if that's what bus fares cost, he guessed he'd have to get used to having less disposable income than he had been used to back home. In all fairness, he couldn't remember the last time he'd actually been on a bus in Alabama. Thinking back, it had probably been a school bus, sometime, way back in the last century.

Otis had dreamed of this day for so long. He was to be based in Lincolnshire for the next academic year, courtesy of a generous research grant that should enable him to bring to fruition one of his oldest and most heartfelt projects. It would be a mistake to call this a "pet" project; this one was a "beast". If he could support his tentative theories with evidence from the field (or "fields" in the case of Lincolnshire) then he would surely make an indelible mark on the history and origins of popular music; indeed, the very foundations of western popular culture itself. These thoughts literally made him tingle with excitement, though, in part, that was also due to the vibrations of the train. The American word "boxcar" seemed eerily apt for this rattling contraption.

As the train approached the county town, he was struck by the magnificence and scale of the building on top of the ridge. Surely, the famous Lincoln Cathedral. A little further along, there seemed to be a castle.

Wow, thought Otis, *this is really old. Certainly nothing remotely like this back home in Alabama.*

Otis was met at the railway station – another quaint old stone building – by a young woman from the university's HR department, who whisked him away in a cab to the University of Lindum accommodation that he was to occupy for the next year. The "flat", as she called it, was quite spartan, but he was pleased to notice that it boasted a fine view of the cathedral up on the hill. As he took possession of the keys, a great wave of exhaustion overcame him, and very soon his head hit the pillow for the first time ever in Lincolnshire, and he fell into a deep and prolonged sleep.

Sunday was spent mostly sleeping, but Monday Otis had a meeting arranged for ten. He was to meet Professor Jim Wilson, who had spent much of the previous three months emailing Otis with arrangements for his working schedule in Lincolnshire.

Otis was shown to his office which he noticed didn't have a view of the cathedral but instead a rather busy branch of McDonald's (maybe they were trying to make him feel at home?).

Next up, Otis was to meet the head of the school and be introduced to the team of researchers that had agreed to work on his project. Most of those were PhD students, whose own work overlapped with Otis's specific areas of study.

Otis handed out his cards to everyone present: Professor of Comparative Anthropology (Music and Popular Culture). This underlined his particular specialism. As soon as he did this, however, he realised he would have to get new ones printed for this year. It would be no good people trying to contact him on his Alabama telephone number...

As agreed in the email exchanges, the county had already been divided into several geographical areas, and Otis was going out into the fields, gathering data, resources and evidence relevant to the study. Each of the main areas had already been allocated a researcher, who had been tasked with providing Otis with general background research, and a suggested list of key people who might be of benefit to the study.

Otis was a great believer in serendipity and had frequently found that following one's own nose often led to the most interesting findings. He had a voluminous knowledge of American popular music and popular culture. He knew that some of the original US settlers, the Pilgrim Fathers who sailed on *The Mayflower*, had originated from Lincolnshire. He was keen to see if there were any parallel developments in music and popular culture in these two similar, largely rural, communities.

Otis had become fascinated with England and its history after a high school lesson about the Pilgrim Fathers, and their journey away from Europe and its religious intolerance. It had always struck him what an amazing thing it was to have upped sticks, organised a boat, and sailed across the wide Atlantic Ocean into the wilds of America; what a major, life-changing decision, to remove oneself and one's family from all things familiar and to step out into the unknown.

One thing that really interested Otis the academic historian, was what cultural influences these people brought with them. In order to do this, he needed to explore, in detail, the world they had left behind, hence this trip to England. The place names in the New World could clearly be seen to reflect places in the Old World: New York/old York; Manchester in Vermont and New Hampshire; a Warwick, a Worcester and, of course, Boston. There was a Richmond and a Norfolk in

Virginia, and a Durham in North Carolina. He thought there were probably thousands of other places too, not to mention the many Lincolns (though most of those seemed to be down to Abe rather than the country town of Lincolnshire). However, as Otis was fond of telling his research students back home, you never knew what you'd find until you started digging...

When Otis had spoken to British academics at international conferences, most of them couldn't think of any significant musical connections with Lincolnshire at all. In fact, most of them tended to say that Lincolnshire was a bit of a backwater, largely known for its agriculture – particularly cabbages and potatoes – but not a great deal more.

Well, here he was, and he was going into the fields of Lincolnshire to start digging! If his hypothesis was correct, he was hoping to find much more than potatoes in this rich, fertile ground. He couldn't wait to get started.

CHAPTER 2

The First Team Meeting: Down to Work

The next morning, Otis convened the first team meeting of the year. He introduced himself, and finally met the team of researchers that had been assigned to his project. He was flattered to learn that some of them had done some research into his background, and several people were clearly familiar with his published work.

Now then, as they tended to say rather a lot in Lincolnshire, *down to business.*

For research purposes, the county had already been divided into several distinct areas for the purpose of convenience: Gainsborough and the north, Louth, Boston and Greater Brassica to the south, Stamford, Lincoln, Market Rasen, Grimsby.

Other work was to focus on the Great Western Festival of 1972, and the mysterious 'Vinyl Triangle' in the deep south of the region.

Otis was at pains to stress that it was music and popular

culture that he was interested in. He was keen to see how it had developed there, in the time since the Pilgrim Fathers had left the country to go and settle in the Americas.

Peter Poker, a PhD student researcher, outlined what he said was quite a sophisticated computer programme, to explore the geographical place names in order to establish links with the county's musical past. He said the work was going well and initial results should be available later in the day.

Poker spent much of his time, if truth be told, studying remarkably expensive models of bicycles and designer Lycra on his desktop. However, in those brief moments between eyeballing the Rapha website, and increasingly ingenious Campagnolo groupsets, he had come up with some useful initial findings.

A schedule of visits was formulated, and Otis was keen to get started. Poker went out to the print room to collect the printout. About fifteen minutes later, he burst into the room. So keen was he to deliver the first fruits of their research, that he had forgotten to remove his bicycle clips (black reflective carbon fibre jobbies – £120 each, from Rapha, of course).

'I really think we're onto something here,' he said, slapping, with a grand flourish, the sizeable document onto the desk in front of Otis. He then excitedly ran through the document, having already highlighted certain key words to convey his main findings.

'BRASSica, the old Roman name for the fenland part of the county,' he said, 'clearly has musical overtones.' Other clues were spread more widely across the county, which clearly pleased Otis: SAXilby, HORNcastle, HARPswell, SAXby, BASSingham. The Isle of AXEholme to the north created some real excitement, what with "axe" being the age-old term for the heavy metal instrument, *par excellence*.

Possible Iron Age connections there, thought Otis.

Searches for links with earlier musical instruments proved a little more difficult to establish. The computer had thrown up Ewerby near Sleaford, which puzzled Otis, till it was explained that "ewer" was an old English word for a jug. There definitely used to be jug bands in earlier times. *Well worth looking into that jug,* thought Otis.

HARMston could refer to harmonica, but Otis thought it unlikely, just as trying to link The Wash to washboard seemed stretching things a little bit too far. It has been suggested that Lutton near Spalding could signify "lute", but that was speedily dismissed as everyone knew that the lute had originally come from Luton in Bedfordshire. Current research pointed to a site somewhere between the airport and the Vauxhall car plant.

Otis wrapped up the meeting as he was keen to read some of the briefing papers prepared for him by the team. He said goodbye to them and then settled down to study a map of the whole county. He was struck by the absence of large conurbations. The map was dotted with many small villages and a number of small towns but only one city – Lincoln – in the whole county, and that was pretty small, as cities went.

His mind wandered back to Northwest Alabama – the place he knew best of all. It was mainly rural with small communities. He'd grown up in Muscle Shoals, a place of about 20,000 people. When linked with the three neighbouring communities of Sheffield, Florence and Tuscumbia, the Quad Cities were known locally as "The Shoals", and totalled nearly 200,000 people today.

Music had, for some reason, become really important in this part of Northwest Alabama. As early as 1873, the great bluesman, WC Handy, had been born in Florence. He was known as the "Father of the Blues" and his *St Louis Blues* is one of the most famous of all jazz tunes. There is an annual WC Handy festival held in the Shoals area to this day.

The siting of a number of recording studios in the 1950s and 1960s had attracted many major stars to this otherwise insignificant part of the rural South. Many great songs had started life in Otis's hometown. When local boy Arthur Alexander recorded *You Better Move On* in Rick Hall's FAME studios in 1961, who would have believed that a little-known English group called The Rolling Stones would record it in 1963, in London, thousands of miles away? Or, that another of Arthur's songs, *Anna*, would appear on The Beatles' first album "Please, Please Me", again, recorded in London in 1963?

Bob Dylan covered the first song Arthur ever recorded – *Sally Sue Brown* – and Elvis Presley had his last US top ten hit with another Arthur Alexander song: *Burning Love*.

Otis thought it wasn't bad that a guy who most people had never heard of from North Alabama, had been the only artist to have had his work covered by The Beatles, The Rolling Stones, Dylan, and Elvis.

Otis thought looking at the map was one thing, but that was only half the story. He wondered if he would discover fascinating insights into Lincolnshire's musical past. In truth, was there much to discover? Then, his mind wandered back to Northwest Alabama. Who would have believed that the self-same Rolling Stones would have gone all that way to record in Muscle Shoals? Or Rod Stewart, Bob Dylan, Paul Simon, Joe Cocker or George Michael, to name but a few?

Songs that have kick-started parties all over the world came out of Otis's humble hometown: *Mustang Sally*, *Land of a 1000 Dances*, and *Sweet Soul Music*. Soulful love ballads like Aretha's *I Never Loved a Man*, or Percy Sledge's *When a Man Loves a Woman*, also came out of this sleepy southern town. Otis really did believe that you didn't see until you started looking. Research could be a very cruel mistress. When things were going well, everything seemed so easy and it all seemed to fall into place, but on those days when things didn't work out, the only recourse was to go back and start again.

There was always a sense of heightened anticipation at the start of a new project, especially one like this, thought Otis, that had been for so long only a figment of his imagination. Now that he was here, in a land far from home, with funding and research assistants in place, he felt the excitement, but also a great sense of responsibility. He was sure that he was going to find much of significance here, but as with any fieldwork, there were always, at the back of his mind, these niggling doubts... Are we asking the right questions? Are we meeting the right people? And are we looking in the right places?

Tomorrow, he would start his quest, and Gainsborough was to be the first port of call. *Bring it on!* he thought.

CHAPTER 3

Gainsborough – Sunday All Week Long

Before setting out on his first field trip to Gainsborough, Otis had done some basic background reading in order to acquire a working overview of the town. It was clearly evident that the place seemed to be well past its golden years, when cruise ships used to sail down the mighty Trent, disgorging thousands of tourists, hungry for culture, designer boutiques and the plethora of Michelin-starred restaurants that lined the once fashionable waterfront. Alas, according to one guidebook, the town had fallen on harder times and, evidently, there were parts of town now where even the pigeons flew upside down because there was nothing worth soiling.

However, Otis was not deterred and, as an experienced field researcher, he wanted to see the place first-hand. He had been planning this trip for so long back home in the South that he could hardly believe he was finally here.

Gainsborough, he had learned, was an old and venerable settlement that had clearly seen better days. His first sighting of the town rather confirmed this. It was mid-week, but the place most definitely had a Sunday feel to it.

Nowadays, its heart had been ripped out, and it was a ghost of its former self. The centre was now called Marshall's Yard, a collection of "retail opportunities", arranged around a car park. Some of the stores seemed empty. The centre's name paid homage to what was once the beating heart of the town – the Marshall factory – site of its major employer. Marshall's workers made powerful engines and agricultural machinery that placed Lincolnshire at the cutting edge of nineteenth and early twentieth century technology.

One of their ingenious inventions was a small sound box placed at the back of their super acme drills and ploughs that scared the crows and seagulls, so that they always flew into the air when following a tractor. This small but powerful device was believed, by those in the know, to be the inspiration and prototype for Jim Marshall's later refinement: the world-famous Marshall Amp.

Gainsborough has a rather tired and decrepit feel to it these days, but it certainly wasn't always like that. Indeed (and you may find this hard to believe) it was, for a few glorious weeks, the actual capital of England. Not only that (and this is really hard to get your head around) it was simultaneously and at the same time the capital of Denmark! Admittedly, this was only for five weeks in the year 1013, but what a remarkable claim to fame. It was all thanks to the Danish king, Sweyn Forkbeard, the well-known dyslexic who, with his son Cnut the Great, defeated the Saxon king, Ethelred, to set up home in the centre of Gainsborough.

So again, thought Otis, *Lincolnshire delivers!*

Now to get under the skin and find out about the musical history. The Spanner antennae were, metaphorically, beginning to twitch as he moved towards the River Trent. Otis noticed a man with a lurcher on a piece of string, staring from a bridge into the river below. The Trent, one of England's major (but hardly mighty) rivers, was not a patch on the Mississippi, thought Otis.

Otis struck up a conversation with the man at the other end of the piece of string who told him he was waiting for the next Aegir. Otis thought this must be a bus, but he couldn't see a bus stop. It was then explained that this was in fact a tidal wave, sometimes called the 'Surge Gainsborough' that came from the Humber all the way along the Trent as far as the town. There was mention of the Aegir (or Eagre as it was sometimes called) Surf Club which flourished in the 1960s, run by two brothers from the local laundry near Trinity church – Sid and Ron White – known locally as the Bleach Boys. Evidently, in the '60s, Gainsborough had quite a sizeable surfer and slacker community, but that's long since gone. Sadly, as yet, no photographic evidence had surfaced of their epic, daring, and dangerous activities, which is probably just as well given modern youth's capacity to indulge in copycat behaviour.

Otis wandered back into town and, feeling somewhat peckish, he popped into a baker's having seen a magnificent display of Lincolnshire plum bread in the shop window. Otis felt it helped get into the spirit of a place if he could sample the local delicacies.

On hearing his southern accent, the staff asked him where he was from. Handing him his plum bread, they told him he was really going to enjoy it.

'Mind you,' said Doris, the oldest of the people serving, 'you'll have to go some to like it as much as that Robert Stigwood.'

'I beg your pardon?' said Otis. 'Did you say Robert Stigwood, the music impresario and manager?'

'He was Australian,' said Doris. 'Used to come up north looking for boy bands, he told us. He said he'd found The Bee Gees, and was on the lookout for more. Loved our plum bread, he couldn't get enough of it. We had to send it to London every week. He was a bit of a plum bread addict – we call them plum bread-heads round here.'

'Did he come more than once?' asked Otis.

'Oh yes, quite a few times. The last time, he was on his way to Lincoln to audition a band called Eden. They were the Poole brothers, and they were really brothers – still are, as far as I know! Originally Darren, James and Mark, they changed their names to Ben, Brayford and Paddling. I believe they did have some limited success – had a record deal with Polydor, same label as The Bee Gees – but that's just about where the similarities end. It's rumoured that Ben haunts Lincoln's magnificent cathedral to this day; sometimes even dressing up as Jesus. It's strange how a little success can go to some people's heads. The others still perform, from time to time, at local tea dances, and the family opened a shop selling tea so that there would never be a shortage of that most reviving of afternoon beverages.'

Otis finally managed to extricate himself and his plum bread from the shop. He was feeling thirsty so he entered one of Gainsborough's pubs. He was asked if he wanted "real" ale. *As opposed to a hypothetical one?* he thought. *Oh well, when in England...* So he ordered a pint of real ale. It did cross his mind to ask someone about this "real" ale. What was "real" about it? After all, an ice-cold, long-necked Bud was real enough for him, especially when he had an Alabama thirst on.

Otis had a ploughman's lunch. (The ploughman wasn't too pleased, saying he'd only popped out for a fag, which startled Otis even more till someone explained.)

In order to let the food settle, Otis went for a short walk to the north of the town centre and came to the wonderful Gainsborough Old Hall, easily the grandest building in town. He was sure that its minstrels' gallery in the Great Hall had witnessed some wonderful musicians in centuries long ago. He vaguely wondered what a hurdy-gurdy sounded like but, then again, he couldn't believe for a second that anyone would have one in Lincolnshire today.

As Otis rounded a corner, he discovered that he was far from the first visitor Gainsborough Old Hall had hosted from the southern states. He read a notice informing him that on

October fourth 1855, a certain William Craft had given a talk about his escape from a slave plantation in Georgia.

That's even before the war between the states! thought Otis. Evidently, William and his wife Ellen, a pale-skinned slave on account of being the illegitimate daughter of the plantation owner, had escaped and taken a ship from Savannah up north to Boston, and freedom. In order to avoid the notorious slave-catchers who would try to return them to what some believed to be their "rightful owners", they migrated to England. A wholly understandable situation in the circumstances, Otis surmised, but at the same time somewhat ironic, given that the plantations and the mass importation of slave workers had largely been down to British capital and the brutal efficiency of British traders.

Otis stood in the very same room that William had lectured in over 170 years ago. He thought, *some things about our history are not as edifying as others...*

After this sombre interlude, Otis thought it better to get back to the task in hand. So far, the morning had yielded very little. He had been hoping for something more tangible. Still, he had the rest of the day.

A trick he had learned when such field trips weren't going well was to explore the local thrift or charity shops. In any community of any reasonable size, these shops always appeared; places where people deposited their surplus unwanted stuff. They also usually stocked old vinyl records which to a trained researcher like Otis told many stories of the past.

A quick flick through the vinyl albums usually gave Otis a sound finger on the local musical pulse. Unfortunately, the pulse was faint to non-existent; the usual diet of Jim Reeves, Mantovani, Slim Whitman, Cliff Richard, Val Doonican, Mrs Mills and Des O'Connor were all there. As the penultimate record cover fell forward, it revealed an album that caught Otis's eye. A black and white gatefold sleeve, its title *Galactic Zoo Dossier* leaped out in bold black letters and underneath it said *Kingdom Come*, and beneath that, in smaller letters still, it said: Arthur Brown. The front cover had side and front "mugshots" of four band members, with a list of personal details. *Very unusual*, Otis thought, but even with his extensive musical knowledge, he didn't recognise anyone at all.

On opening the gatefold cover, there was a colourful collage á la Kurt Schwitters that could easily have graced a Frank Zappa or Brian Eno album. Upon looking at the back, Otis found something that made him smile: three more band "mugshots". One was Arthur Brown himself, or Arthur Wilton Brown to give him his full name, born in Whitby, Yorkshire. This was the man who had a chart single in 1968 with a song called *Fire*, produced by Pete Townsend of The Who. This single had one of the most alarming openings ever, with Brown declaring in his demonic dark-brown voice: "I am the God of hellfire and I bring you fire!" He once performed wearing a flaming helmet, and proceeded to set fire to himself, almost burning his hair off.

But it wasn't Brown's satanic, Manson-like "mugshot" that brought back Otis's smile: it was the picture of the younger and much smaller lead guitarist Andrew Kenneth Dalby that really excited Otis. Directly underneath the "mugshot", it read: *Place of birth – Gainsborough.*

At last, thought Otis, *a real lead, and a real lead guitarist!* This was a breakthrough and Otis, on handing over his fifty pence piece, became the proud owner of one of the jewels of British prog-rock.

The album even contained its original poster with lyrics and a picture of Arthur on a crucifix. *What is it about this place?* wondered Otis. *That's two musicians with Jesus complexes in one day!*

A quick word in Mr Google's ear had provided Otis with more information to follow up: Andy Dolby was still playing and recording music today.

Another thing Otis always tried to do was to enlist the help of local specialists. He went into the Gainsborough library, and eventually someone asked him what he wanted. He told the female assistant briefly about his area of research and his interest in Lincolnshire's musical past.

Otis was told to wait and she said she'd bring the reference librarian.

'He knows everything about Gainsborough, he'll help you out. He's a god around these parts. What he doesn't know about Gainsborough's not worth knowing.'

She returned and introduced Otis to Mr English. Otis

reflected that in all his years in the US, he'd never once encountered a Mr American.

Mr English's eyes lit up after listening to Otis's brief explanation of his research topic.

'I may be able to help,' he said with an enigmatic smile. 'Gainsborough has a long and interesting musical past. Being on a great river, like Memphis and New Orleans, it was always a natural meeting place for artists and especially musicians.'

He told of how in the '50s and '60s the great Scunny Boy Williamson would come down from the steel town up north, and play with the likes of Long John Bawtry, and Alexis and Caenby Korner. His eyes went positively misty, when he recalled a show by the one and only John Lee Humber and Screamin' Jay Hykeham. There had been a thriving blues scene in the town.

'I think we may have a few field recordings in the stacks in the basement, if you can spare me a few minutes to see what I can find?'

Otis was so excited he wanted to join Mr English, but he realised that he must not behave in an unprofessional manner.

Mr English returned, somewhat dusty, carrying several boxes containing old tape reels of dubious vintage. He also produced several boxes of cassettes, saying that there had been an attempt in the early 80s to transfer many of the old tapes to this more modern format for ease of listening. He then produced an early Sony Walkman, saying Otis would be able to borrow it as he was clearly engaged in genuine local historical research. Otis couldn't believe his good fortune; he asked Otis if he had the old technology to play the material that hadn't been put onto cassette. Otis assured him that the tech people at the university loved challenges of this sort.

The first box contained gems by Lightning Horncastle, Witham Willie Dixon, Saxilby Slim, Little Walter and his dad Big Walter, Plum Bread Pete, King Biscuit Boy and Blind Lemon Jaffa Cake.

Another box revealed more hidden gems, and a real surprise: a true American legend, on a rare and very early trip to the UK, to find long lost family – Muddy Waters and his brother, Burton Waters. Other 'gems' included Big Bill Bardney, Little Kesteven, and not forgetting Nat King Coleby and Leadenham Belly.

Yet a further box revealed some of the great female artists who used to belt it out in the Lincolnshire of old: Sister Rosetta Rasen, Mable Thorpe, Donna Nook, and a special performance by sisters Haslet and Ruth Brawn, singing their big hit *Chine On, Harvest Moon*. Mr English produced a photo of these two seriously "meaty" women.

Truly formidable, thought Otis.

Another tape was labelled The Pot Shop Boys – personal favourites of Mr English, he said – Sid and Eric Kettle, whose dad owned the local hardware store on Spital Terrace. Never actually made a record.

'It's a sin, because they were really good well, good for Gainsborough.'

Mr English reached into a folder and brought out a rather brown press cutting from *The Lincolnshire Chronicle*.

'Ah yes,' he said, 'I nearly forgot about this,' and he handed Otis the cutting.

It was believed that Peter Green, the great lead guitarist with Fleetwood Mac, wrote *Black Magic Woman* after buying a box of dark chocolates from a stall on Gainsborough market one Friday on his way to a gig in nearby Retford.

Otis read from the article:

Madge Smith (54) of the Middlefield Estate, who runs the sweet stall on the market, recalls: 'I could tell from his voice that he wasn't from round here, but he was still very nice. He also asked had we any green manalishis, but unfortunately I'd just sold the last ones that morning.

"A pity", he said, as he was very partial to them.

I said, 'Try the Co-op, or Albert Ross the newsagent's – they might have some.' But I don't know whether he could be bothered. It's quite a trek up there'.

'That reminds me,' said Mr English, warming to his topic. 'In the early '60s there was a local act that caused quite a stir: Don and Phil Smart from Lea, just on the edge of town. Their dad, Ted, owned the garage near Lea Road Station. Those boys lived up to their name Smart and went to the local grammar school. The Clever Lea Brothers, they were called. They had a song called *Wake up Little Floosie* about staying out too late and missing the last train back from Sheffield. Caused a lot of trouble it did. It was banned down the local youth club. Only became a hit because people went out to buy it to burn copies of it. I reckon it would have been banned on local radio too, but back then there wasn't such a thing in Gainsborough.'

This reminded Otis of his Uncle Wilbur back home in Huntsville, who had put on what the kids called his "ghost suit", and had lit a bonfire to burn all Otis's Beatles records. Again, Otis was seeing that some things were pretty common all over the world.

Evidently, The Clever Lea Brothers were keen anglers, and they had another hit record called *Loose Eel*. That one wasn't banned in youth clubs, thankfully.

Mr English went on to explain, in case Otis didn't know, that Sheffield, a large steel city in south Yorkshire, was only a short train journey away; near enough for some Sheffield acts to pop over to Gainsborough from time to time to play in the local pubs and working men's clubs. Joe Cocker and his lad, Jarvis, both played there at different times. Very popular with the grammar school crowd, that Jarvis Cocker and the Spaniels. Phil Oakley, from The Human League, came over once to have his hair cut, but he had to leave halfway through to catch the last train back.

While Otis was taking all this new information in, Mr English let slip the fact that some of the original Pilgrim Fathers came from very near here, just across the Trent in Nottinghamshire. They had joined up with the Gainsborough

Separatists and went to Boston hoping to get a boat to Holland, which a lot of Gainsborough folk evidently did. Eventually though many sailed on *The Mayflower* from Plymouth and settled in Massachusetts. Otis thanked him for this small history lesson and started to pack up his things. Mr English gave him a form so he could borrow the old tapes.

Just as Otis was thanking Mr English for his invaluable assistance, the reference librarian threw in what Otis could only call "a curveball".

'Well, I suppose you know Gainsborough's Michael Jackson connection?'

Otis did a double-take! 'Michael Jackson? *The* Michael Jackson? The self-styled King of Pop? You mean *that* Michael Jackson?'

There was an impressive pause as the reference librarian raised himself to his full height, smiled, and nodded. 'I agree, it's a fairly ordinary name, but yes, I do mean that self-same Michael Jackson, though I'm not sure the "king of pop" title goes down too well around here. Most people regard R. White as the king of pop in these parts.'

This last statement went over Otis's head. Still, he was keen to hear about this Jackson connection,

'Well,' said Mr English, warming to his task, 'Quincey Jones visited Japan in the early 1980s and really liked a song by the YMO, the Yellow Magic Orchestra, a band from Tokyo formed by Ryuichi Sakamoto and two friends. The song was called *Behind the Mask* and had lyrics by a Tokyo-based British musician called Chris Mosdell. Chris was born in Gainsborough! Jackson slightly reworked the lyrics, and was planning to include the track on his forthcoming album *Thriller*. Because of legal wrangling about sharing royalties, the track never made the album, only to surface twenty-five years later as a Michael Jackson single. Oh, and a certain Eric Clapton also recorded the song on his album *August* in 1986.'

Otis was amazed. Lincolnshire had come up trumps again! Who would have guessed that sleepy old Gainsborough had links with Michael Jackson and old Slowhand himself?

The reference librarian could see the effect he had had on Otis. He was enjoying this. 'Of course, there is a much greater Lincolnshire connection with Michael Jackson than Chris Mosdell's modest link...'

'Now, hold your horses,' said Otis. 'What do you mean?'

'Two words,' teased the reference librarian, who hadn't had this much fun in years. 'Rod Temperton!'

Otis, who was by now in a state of shock said, 'Red Temperature?'

'No!' said the reference librarian. 'Rod Temperton, the Lincolnshire songwriter extraordinaire who went to school in Market Rasen and came from the Grimsby area.'

'You mean the Heatwave – *Boogie Nights* guy?' said Otis, thinking that "Red Temperature" wasn't too far off the mark in the circumstances.

'Yes, the very same,' said the now gleeful reference librarian, who was having one of his best days in many a long month. 'It's clear to me that if you're going to become Lincolnshire's Pevsner of pop, you have a great deal more in-depth research to do. To misquote the late Karen Carpenter: "You've only just begun". Oh, and by the way, I believe she has no connection with The Carpenters Arms pub in Fiskerton, before you start getting carried away.'

Otis, who had now collapsed into a heap on the floor, was desperately trying to take all this in. He couldn't believe his good fortune. This was what he was coming to love about Lincolnshire – its infinite capacity to surprise. Its very ordinariness hid the most remarkable secrets; you only needed to know where to look.

Otis was advised to drive back to Lincoln a different way. Mr English told him to drive via Stow as there had been reports of mystical stirrings in what was locally known as Etherwood. At times, locals have noticed an insistent drum and bass sound wafting through the air. Some folks say there are "hippy types" living in vans which emit very fast rhythmic beats (probably been on that neon dust or the magic mushrooms that dot the fields around here). Otis made a mental note to follow this up later.

Otis drove back to the Lindum campus with the song *Boogie Nights* going round in his head. Unfortunately, the only two words he could remember were "boogie" and "nights", but that couldn't stop the feeling of elation, and the sense that he was on the cusp of further great discoveries. So now the net had widened to Grimsby.

'This is going so much better than I'd anticipated,' he said to himself out loud. He was one of the very few people who could genuinely say that they were looking forward to a trip to Grimsby.

CHAPTER 4

A Most Unexpected Trip to London

As Otis was writing up his experiences in Gainsborough, he was interrupted by a call from his Head of School. The usual pleasantries ensued: "Hope you're settling in. Glad to hear the field visits have started." Then she cut to the real purpose of the call.

'The vice chancellor has asked me to invite you to take her place at a consultation meeting in London tomorrow, as she has been called away at short notice. She thinks it will be of interest to you, given your knowledge of Gainsborough.'

Otis was somewhat puzzled by this, but was clearly impressed by how these guys seemed to be really on the ball.

Evidently, the government has a new policy about spreading resources more fairly across the nation. Given the poorest states back home were all in the south it struck a chord with Otis. The proposal was to channel investment and resources to these areas that had often been neglected in the past. The government claimed it was committed to "levelling up", as they called it; an end to the old habit of spending billions on roads and infrastructure in London and the southeast, and sending a couple of trucks up to Lincolnshire to fill in some potholes. It was a way of saying "we haven't forgotten you" to those places that had clearly been forgotten for decades.

So, the idea of building a spanking-new Tate Gallery in Lincolnshire took root. With Tate Britain and Tate Modern in London, the government had already established new Tate galleries in St Ives in Cornwall, and at the Albert Dock in Liverpool. So a Tate gallery in the east of the country seemed a logical next step.

The Lindum University vice chancellor, an art historian of international repute, had been called in on early discussions and had been hoping to attend a consultation meeting with interested stakeholders. At the last minute she had been called away on urgent family business and had asked her PA to get hold of that "interesting visiting American professor" who, as far as she could remember, was an expert on Gainsborough. Thus it was that Otis came to attend one of the strangest meetings of his career.

News of this "levelling up" project had also reached some of the local Brassica county councillors, who had long entertained the idea of a major visitor attraction in what they felt was a neglected and forgotten part of the county. This Tate gallery proposal was just what they wanted, and they ran with it, immediately instructing officers to draw up plans for the new Tate gallery. Imagine being finally on the map after being ignored and overlooked for so long! And, what's more, a gallery/museum dedicated to the county's main contribution to the rest of the country – the great Lincolnshire potato, or "tate" as it's known in these parts. Galleries would be dedicated to the history and versality of this noble tuber; a palace fit for King Edwards; earlies, second-earlies, main crop – such a great variety – the public would love it. Charlotte, Nicola, and Desirée – they all had great stories to tell.

So many ideas just leaped off the page – galleries of designer jacket potatoes, amazing creative fillings, the history of the chip from fat, triple-fried, hand-cut to skinny French fries, roast tates, rosti, gnocchi, crisps, even. Maybe the Walkers Gallery in Liverpool could loan some exhibits. It was also planned to get some of those big Henry Moore potato sculptures. Mind you, they were a bit pricey. (You don't get many of them to the pound these days.)

There was great excitement about the interactive gallery where folks could actually buy chips and eat them! How avant-garde was that? A gallery where the art was produced for daily consumption. What a wonderful opportunity to showcase some of the delicacies of the Brassica region.

Otis had been given a sheaf of papers to read on the gallery proposals, and a first-class ticket to London on the direct seven a.m. train.

The whole of the first class carriage had been booked for the Lincolnshire stakeholders to travel to the meeting, with officials from the "levelling up" project based in the Cabinet Office.

Otis was feeling a little out of his comfort zone, if truth be told. He found himself sitting opposite a local MP who, judging by the conversation he couldn't help overhearing, had just been promoted to a junior position in the Ministry of Agriculture.

Well, at least that makes sense, thought Otis, *given the county's main line of business.* He'd read somewhere that Lincolnshire produces just over an eighth of total UK food. Sitting next to the rookie minister was a senior civil servant from the ministry. He had clearly come to take the new boy under his wing, as they had, the previous day, completed a whistle-stop tour of some of the key players in the county's vast agribusiness community. The young, new junior minister was what could only be described as "bright-eyed and bushy-tailed", brimming with enthusiasm. It was hard for the man from the ministry to get a word in.

'So, let me get this clear: you buy a bulb of garlic, break it up into individual cloves, plant each clove into the ground and "hey presto", each single clove turns into a bulb? Well, that's remarkable! Who else knows about this? I can see great potential here. I mean, this has real implications for solving the world's food crisis. I don't suppose this system works for other stuff, does it? That would be too much to hope for. If it does, believe you me, I think we could have a winner on our hands here!'

Otis hardly dared look at the unflappable civil servant who said, keeping a very straight face, 'Sir, I think the French might have an inkling about this garlic business...'

'Typical,' the new man replied, 'but what makes you say this?'

'Let's just call it "nasal intuition", Minister. Still, I'm sure the Secretary of State would be only too happy to receive new ideas from his new junior agriculture minister. Shall I set up an appointment with his private secretary?'

'Right away, no time to waste. This could revolutionise the foreign aid we give to the Third World. I mean, if we could drop say a million bulbs of garlic in a famine zone, within a year they could have oh, maybe fifteen million. Goodness, these things breed like rabbits... Now there's an idea!'

Otis could see the older man with his head in his hands, as his new charge ploughed on.

'Do we in the ministry deal with er living things – what are they called, animals? Or are we just plants?'

'There are, I believe, a large number of what could loosely be termed "vegetables" under our control, but yes, sir, animals are part of our national responsibility!'

'Well, there we are, then! We could send rabbits as well, and pretty soon they'd have more than they'd know what to do with. After all, rabbits breed like—'

'Indeed, they do, Minister. May I ask, what would the rabbits live on in the famine zone?'

'Indeed, I see your point. If we're not careful, they might

eat the rabbits before they could do the business so to speak, or the rabbits might eat the garlic. We can't have that. We shall have to draft regulations, put it into law, even, stating that we can't be dropping rabbits where we are already dropping garlic. Good thinking! I'm really enjoying the challenge of working in this department already!'

'Well, I'm glad to hear that, Minister. I'm sure your tenure will be a great success; a launch pad to greater things, no doubt. I'm sure the great offices of state are, even now, preparing themselves for your future elevation.'

'Gosh, do you really think so?'

'Well, all in good time, Minister, but now, let's focus on the outbreak of cabbage blight in Brassica, shall we?'

'I suppose we must...'

As the train moved through Newark, Otis left his own personal purgatory behind, and put on his headphones to listen to some of the music that Mr English had unearthed from the dusty vaults in the Gainsborough archives. *A bit of Screaming Jay Hykeham, the king of the suburban blues, should hit the spot*, he mused.

Having entered his own world for the rest of the journey, Otis found himself in a much better mood. As Desirée and Maris Piper's sultry version of *I Only Have Eyes for You* came to an end, so did the journey. King's Cross once more.

The train was on time, and everyone was led to a fleet of cars that moved off, not to the original Whitehall venue, but to a large impressive building on the south bank of the Thames:

Tate Modern. Otis found himself wedged between two large, ruddy-faced councillors who, given the pervasive aroma of damp cabbage, were obviously from the deepest and dampest parts of south Brassica.

Two presentations were made by the director of the Tate and the senior minister dealing with the "levelling up" agenda. When it came to questions, it was clear that there was some disquiet amongst the councillors and farming community. Let's just say that one could hear the sound of many pennies beginning to drop.

'So, this here place is an art gallery and it used to be a power station? Have I got that right?' one of the bolder farmers said.

'Indeed,' intoned the minister, and there were nods all around.

'Well, from what I've seen on the walls around here so far, you'd get better value for money if you turned it back into a power station and burnt all this rubbish! Art? You call this art? Young kids in our primary schools churn out better stuff than this, potato printing! Even I can trace better than some of these efforts. Are you telling me that this new Tate gallery in Lincolnshire is going to be an *art* gallery? Do you not know Lincolnshire? Do you think that's what we need, in deepest Brassica? You know nowt. What we want is a quality visitor attraction to bring folks in. Art gallery? Where on earth are you coming from?'

There was a smattering of applause then quite a long pause before the minister for "levelling up" stood up and thanked

Councillor Frank Dogdyke for his spirited contribution, which would certainly be given all due consideration at the next round of meetings later in the day back at the ministry.

Other councillors, wary of losing government investment, made placatory noises, saying the council had already granted outline planning permission for the project and couldn't wait to get down to details.

The other councillor, who had wedged Otis into the corner of the taxi, stood up as the meeting was drawing to a close, and said, 'And what about our potholes?'

Otis was, by now, totally perplexed as to why this day had been inflicted upon him. He did note though how similar some of the local politicians in Brassica were to the backwoodsmen at home in Alabama. There weren't too many rural art galleries in his home state, he had to admit.

On the train journey back, the farming contingent cracked open a crate of Bateman's triple XB and drowned their sorrows. Otis took the opportunity to talk to some of them about their area and recollections of their youth. Frank was moaning that Brassica was not like it was in the good old days.

'It's not like the old days – everything's changing. You can even get French bread now, and the cake shops have started selling Danish pastries and Swiss rolls. Only last week, I saw an Eccles cake. I mean, for goodness' sake, where's that come from?'

Otis was inclined to say "Eccles", but he didn't know where that was, so he held his tongue.

Fred's fellow councillor warmed to the task saying, 'I ordered a ploughman's lunch in Mick's last week, and it came with a Scotch egg. I was bloody furious. I sent it back and gave that barman a right flea in his eye. I said, if I want a bloody Scotch egg, I'll go to Scotchland! Times are changing, all right; it's not like it used to be round here. I don't like it one little bit...'

There was a chorus of agreement.

Otis seized his moment to steer the conversation round to their musical experiences, which gave him a taste of what he was in for when he went on his next fieldtrip to Boston and Brassica. He kept hearing people talk about the "Gliderdrome" and a "kind of Irish, but not Irish bar", called Cultural Mick's. It all sounded fascinating, and he vowed that he would start his research on this place, in earnest, the very next day.

CHAPTER 5

Boston: The Capital of Brassica and Cultural Mick's

When Otis arrived in his office the next day, he immediately asked one of his research assistants for the file they had been putting together on the Boston Gliderdrome. When it appeared on his desk, he could not believe how thick it was and what riches it contained. He'd been led to believe that Boston was a bit of a backwater – a forgotten place of no interest to anyone – but how wrong he was.

As Otis thumbed through the file, he was totally poleaxed by the quality of what was before his eyes. The cream of the British pop scene of the '60s and early '70s played here (though to be pedantic, only two thirds of Cream actually made it up to Boston, but that's another story).

What was even more fascinating to Otis, as an American music fan, was the number of US performers who had entertained crowds in this sleepy part of Lincolnshire. Evidently, there had first been an ice rink and, in 1964, a performing space was added next to it called the Starlight

Rooms. Little Miss Dynamite Brenda Lee, Solomon Burke, Otis Redding and Lee Dorsey had all played there.

Holy cow! thought Otis. *It gets even better!* In 1967 the Jimi Hendrix Experience came to town, as did another of the all-time greats: Stevie Wonder! 1968 saw Ike and Tina Turner hit Boston, which must have made a change as reports later showed that it was usually Ike hitting Tina that made the news.

The Ronettes, the Platters, and Motown's Jimmy Ruffin all performed there, and in 1970 two soul divas, Carla (*Tramp*) Thomas and Fontella (*Rescue Me*) Bass, breezed in. Otis felt he had struck gold. There couldn't be many venues in London, LA, or New York that could boast such a roster of artists.

The list of British artists was equally amazing, running the whole gamut from The Animals to Yes, in 1972. Solo artists like Tom Jones and Dusty Springfield also played the Starlight Rooms, alongside many group recording artists of the golden age of British pop.

A quick glance confirmed that The Beatles and The Rolling Stones had not found their way to the Gliderdrome, but almost everyone else had. The Animals, the Kinks, the Yardbirds, Them (with the great Van Morrison), the Small Faces, Manfred Mann, Traffic, Procul Harum, Status Quo, T. Rex, Yes, Thin Lizzie, Slade, ELO, Lindisfarne, Curved Air, Elton John, and the Jeff Beck group, with star vocalist a Mr Rod Stewart, no less.

'Not at all bad,' said Otis with a wry smile.

The owner, Sydney Malkinson, claimed he was probably

the only dance promoter who had turned down The Beatles – not the volume, the actual booking. They'd been booked as a support act in their early days, but he cancelled the booking because he thought £35 was too much for an unknown band that *he* hadn't even heard of...

The story goes that Brian Epstein rang to change the date, but Sydney cancelled the booking. It's ironic that when the proposed rearranged gig came around, The Beatles were top of the charts. And the rest is history!

Some acts were so popular they played more than once. In fact, Roy Wood played the venue in three different bands: the Move, then ELO, and finally with Wizzard.

Boston clearly had a large number of Motown and soul fans, judging by the top names that came to play there.

It was reported in a local paper that the lead singer with the Jeff Beck group, Rod Stewart, had a kickabout before their gig on the nearby Boston United football ground. When he played with The Faces, he often had kickabouts on stage too. Indeed, after becoming a global superstar, Rod built his own full-sized football pitch next to his Essex mansion.

There was a well-established pattern of successful rock stars indulging in their favourite pastimes. It kept them grounded. Not many people knew that Sid Vicious was a chess grandmaster and that he had a solid gold chess set for special occasions. Actually, he had another everyday set with hollow pieces for when he played speed chess with Ozzy Osbourne. Each piece was filled with amphetamines, and when you took a piece, you took the speed. Capturing the queen was always a great high. It could get messy, and it often did,

Otis discovered Ozzy had an idea for a game where both players had black pieces, but he could never understand why it didn't work out. Ozzy said he often played in total darkness to add another level of difficulty. That didn't work out, either. *He's so rock 'n' roll*, thought Otis.

It was fitting, Otis thought that the final gig at the Starlight Rooms was by someone with real Lincolnshire tumbleweed connections – Elton John – with of course material written by Lincolnshire's own Bernie T.

One that got away was chameleon performer, David Bowie. He was booked for June twenty-third 1973, touring as Ziggy Stardust and the Spiders from Mars. However, it was decided to shut the Starlight Rooms down as the venue had suffered such a great deal of vandalism – slashed seats, smashed toilets – the usual mindless stupidity. The management closed it down because they said: "Youngsters are unwilling to accept reasonable discipline, rules, and ordinary standards of behaviour". *Teenage high spirits have a lot to answer for*, thought Otis.

After studying the file in greater detail, Otis discovered that a local researcher had found evidence in the form of a poster that Bowie had in fact played the venue after all. A good few years earlier, aged only nineteen, on August thirteenth 1966 to be precise, he appeared as David Bowie and the Buzz, supporting two former Merseybeats members, John and

Johnny. Otis briefly wondered whatever happened to them.

Otis noticed at the bottom of the poster an advert for forthcoming events: on August twentieth the rather vague All Star Coloured Group and Singers, and on August twenty-seventh, the Small Faces. Otis wondered what colour their small faces might be...

It was only later when a colleague told Otis that one of the most popular British TV shows in the '60s was *The Black and White Minstrel Show*, that he realised what an odd place he had come to work in.

Later that week, Otis finally went in to Boston and undertook serious fieldwork, heartened by the knowledge that the place had hosted so many world-famous musicians. He wanted to get a "feel" for the place and to interview people who had witnessed this musical golden age first-hand.

One name kept coming up: Cultural Mick's, a bar that seemed to have been at the centre of musical life in the town for many decades. Evidently, this was *the* place for after parties. All the great musicians ended up at Mick's. Boston, being a market town, meant that certain pubs could open at unusual hours to cater for workers who worked what were known as "unsocial hours". The same thing applied at the old Covent Garden market in London, where porters who'd worked through the night could get a beer with their breakfast. These special licences meant a more relaxed pace of drinking and the pubs also served food, not always common in the 1960s in the UK. It was reported that Jimi Hendrix loved the bubble and squeak in Mick's so much, he even asked for the recipe.

Dave, a helpful barman, said that many of the US acts were fascinated by the food on offer. They called the ubiquitous Brussels sprouts "junior cabbages" and couldn't get enough of them. Otis Redding said the cabbage from around Spalding way reminded him of collard greens, an old southern soul food favourite.

When Mick set up the bar in the late '50s, he wanted to champion local produce and local ale. Clearly a man well ahead of his time. Mick also welcomed all kinds of people into the bar. His thinking was that he wanted the "vibe" of an Irish bar, but to serve people from all over, hence the name Cultural Mick's. There were many foreign workers in the area, and Mick realised that they needed somewhere to have a drink and call home while cutting cabbages in England. The Boston pub was one of the first anywhere to display clocks showing different times in different cities. Later, when Cultural Mick's became a globally franchised phenomenon, it was reassuring to know that there was always a Mick's open somewhere in the world – Boston, LA, Rio, Zip City, Tokyo, London, Sydney, and Bardney.

Music was always a key element in the mix. Mick had made good friends with an American businessman, Andy Warthog, who had set up a safari park near Boston. It hadn't gone well, and when the rhinos and hippos escaped, the writing was on the wall. Who can forget the *Lincolnshire Echo* headline: *Hippos cause Havoc in the Haven!* Andy moved into band management, and he provided a group of locals who became Cultural Mick's house band.

Andy named them the Vegetable Underground and its leaders, John Kale and singer Blue Reed, really went down a storm. John Kale hailed from Brassica (not to be confused with his cousin JJ Kale – never mix them up, they're very different musically). *What a difference a J makes*, thought Otis.

The Vegetable Underground really developed their own "rootsy" style and eventually had quite a successful career, even playing as far afield as Norfolk, on occasion. Sometimes they'd back artists who had retired to Mick's as they chilled and jammed after hours. Hendrix learned a few local tunes while jamming here, and added *Bourne under a Bad Sign* and *Sitting on Top of the Wolds* to his already, extensive blues repertoire.

There was quite an eclectic music scene in the early days and a lot of country music in the Brassica district. As Otis took in the big-sky landscape he was reminded of "cracker" music from back home – stuff like those duelling banjos in the movie of James Dickey's novel, *Deliverance*. The Brassica fenland communities were small and scattered, with lots of water, drainage channels and dykes, and lots of cabbages. Everywhere cabbages as far as the eye could see. Local jukeboxes would throb to the sound of Johnny Cash-Crop, Butch Dyke and the Fentastic Four and, especially, Mud Flatts and his Boston Banjo Boys. Otis was told that Wayne Fleet and the Mindbenders always went down well in Boston – they played a kind of driving country rock powered by copious quantities of Bateman's Triple XB. A potent mix, if ever there was one.

Mick's welcomes all sorts, as shown by one of the regulars Rus Kington. Rus always cried inside when he heard the words *sometimes it's hard to be a woman* dripping out of the jukebox. Rus, a particularly large-handed transvestite from Fishtoft, and a legend in the potato fields around Boston, had encountered difficulties in every other hostelry in town, but Mick's had taken him in. Mick didn't mind what his customers wore at the weekend, as long as they were buying beer. It's said that many a homesick foreign land worker had been taken in by the surprises to be found lurking under Rus's favoured Laura Ashley floral print frocks. Not for nothing was he nicknamed the Boston Stump in those parts.

Mick made everyone welcome. Before the music took off, he tried a range of initiatives. He even tried "stand up" once, but the regulars complained and demanded that he brought the chairs back. Some were more successful than others. Games night included the world's first dyslexic Scrabble tournament, but judging that was so difficult as there were so many different languages on the go at the same time.

The meat raffles started off well, but leaving the meat on the bar all week was a bit of a turn off, especially in those hot Brassica summers. Eventually, it was decided to place the prize on a cooler window ledge. As people were more likely to buy raffle tickets if they could see the prize, a sign on the bar with an arrow pointing upwards, read: *Meat on the ledge*. It's believed a young Richard Thompson used that as the title for one of his best songs for Fairport Convention.

This proves that inspiration can come from anywhere, thought Otis.

Mick wasn't too happy with this situation though, as there had sometimes been complaints that the meat had "gone off". He solved that problem with the Argentinian nights. The prizes were tins of Fray Bentos steak and kidney pies. The only trouble was no one had a tin opener. These ended up flying round the bar like lethal Frisbees – several people lost teeth that night. It's believed that the increase in the number of UFO sightings in the Boston area can be directly traced to those popular Tuesday nights. After that, the first raffle prize was always the tin opener.

Spam nights were a big hit with the folks who travelled in from Skegness and the Costa Caravana. It was thought that there was an affinity between living in a metal box and eating food out of another metal box. At least they had a balanced meal, it being served with sprouts and presented on a bed of shredded cabbage. There was a house rule: you had to support local industry and eat local produce. You could order with or without cabbage, but whatever the order it always came with cabbage – house rules.

There was a big festival in a field near Bardney in 1972, with a huge line-up of bands, and a first live performance for a comedy novelty act called (rather unfunnily, Otis thought) Monty Python's Flying Circus. Evidently, those lads stopped off at Mick's on the way back to London during a spam night.

It could be a coincidence, but later in their career they had a nice little earner with a spam show of their own. The barman at Mick's said he saw a clip on the news recently about the tall one. They said he'd moved to Torquay, gone mad, and beaten his car up with branches from a tree. Probably did too much spam in his younger days.

Some of the other local pubs tried bingo, but Mick was against gambling, saying he'd seen it ruin too many good men. The local branch of Walkabout introduced Dingo, a game where they let a wild dog loose at about eleven p.m. just to liven things up a bit. Never failed – some of the locals loved it by all accounts.

Incidentally, it was Mick who introduced the sturdy sprout stalk as a weapon with which to keep the peace. All bouncers eventually took up the idea, and it is still very much a tradition carried on in the area today. People laughed at first, but it only took one or two lashes to realise that it was a highly effective – nay, dangerous – weapon in the wrong hands. Now it was the law in Brassica that all bouncers had to undergo an intensive ten-minute training course run by local Brassica martial arts experts, and they had to take theory and practical exams in order to acquire the coveted Sprout Stalk Licence. These people were the very SAS of the bouncing fraternity.

All this information came thick and fast, as Otis talked to people in the market place and in Cultural Mick's. There were a few false starts as he encountered a Latvian land worker who said Boston had been hard to get used to. For example, when he first came, there was a shop called Boots, but it didn't sell boots; another shop called Currys, which didn't sell curry – it sold televisions and fridges. It was all very confusing at first. He said he liked to drink in Cultural Mick's however as they respected you, and played good music.

Indeed, the jukebox there was packed with Brassica classics, from Louise Armstrong's *Water Wonderful World*, almost the fenland national anthem, to Chris from Martin's *Yellow*, the song about the jaundice outbreak at the Pilgrim Hospital in 1957, to mention but two.

As Otis walked around the imposing market place, he noted quite a few stores boarded up. A large British Home Stores was now a pop-up shop selling fireworks. Apparently, in a few weeks' time, he was informed, the Brits had a wild night of bonfires and toffee apples, celebrating the capture of some Yorkshire terrorist who had tried to blow up the Houses of Parliament. Judging from the mood of several people Otis had spoken to today, most now would have been happier if he'd succeeded. Another store, Dorothy Perkins, didn't look at all perky, and Top Shop clearly wasn't top anymore as it was boarded up.

Otis had arranged to meet Councillor Frank Dogdyke in the main square at midday. Otis had met him last week on the trip to London about the now blighted Tate gallery project. Frank had agreed to show Otis around and to introduce him to a few of the Brassica movers and shakers. Otis could see Frank deep in conversation with two men in smart suits, obviously local businessmen judging by appearances.

Frank introduced Otis to the Carvery brothers, Toby and Reg. Toby had opened a successful chain of meat restaurants and his brother Reg, not to be outdone, had opened a chain of veg carveries. To be fair, it had been hard for Reg's business to flourish in the early days, but now with all the vegetarian and vegan stuff, he was making a tidy living. As Reg said, "If you can't make a go of it here where we grow the stuff, you don't deserve to have a business at all". All this, "green this, and green that" was manna from Heaven as far as Reg was concerned. Reg said it never ceased to amaze him where his ideas came from. He gave Otis an example. Reg said he was a real law and order man but oddly, he'd been inspired by these latest revolting people – those extinction rabble-rousers. In among some of their frankly crackpot ideas, Reg had seen a great business opportunity. They'd been asking for more sensitive or "green" policing. This led to Reg taking on Cultural Mick's idea of recycling sprout stalks into police batons. The business, like the sprouts, had grown from there, and Reg was now one of the biggest players in the ethical arms industry, currently supplying twenty-four UK police forces and several Middle Eastern states. He was trying to get export licences for the US, but Brexit had made things difficult. Another line that had come back into production was the good old water cannon. After suffering tear gas, running mascara and smoke bombs, these environmental protesters had been bombarding their MPs, demanding the return of water cannons, as they did so much less damage to our fragile environment.

'Nutters, if you ask me, but great for business,' said Reg.

They decided to go for a spot of lunch at Cultural Mick's. On the way, they passed a chip shop.

Reg said to Otis, 'In Grimsby they serve fish with chips, but it never really caught on here.'

Next, they passed a KFC. *Ah*, thought Otis, *the colonel gets everywhere!* But on closer inspection, there was no smiling Colonel Sanders: just a smiling cartoon cabbage. Kesteven Fried Cabbage – that's what the sign read– another local venture capitalising on the ubiquitous green stuff. The window had great adverts for party buckets of twenty-four deep-fried golden sprout nuggets. *Yum*, thought Otis. There was a big push on desserts this week – Sprout Surprise – surely misnamed, since sprouts featured on every line of the capacious menu.

Sprouts grilled and lovingly drizzled in Fenland honey and enrobed in a slightly green cabbage-infused créme anglaise (custard).

'Yum-yum,' said Otis, but in what he hoped was a slightly ironic way.

Once they entered Cultural Mick's, Otis felt a sense of history envelop him. All around were reminders of the past: Fray Bentos tins wedged into the ceiling; the clocks on the wall telling the time in Mick's all over the world; a few (admittedly broken) guitars framed on the walls, and one from Jimi himself – a slightly charred Telecaster. There were also many framed and rather fading black and white photos of the great and the even greater who had graced this hallowed place over the years. Over everything hung the all-pervasive, dark green smell of cabbage.

Otis saw someone move over to the impressive jukebox by the corner of the bar. He fed some coins into the slot. Otis noticed that all the selections came from the local music section labelled "Country and Eastern", which occupied the first two columns on the face of the machine. The box clicked into life and, after a pause, filled with hisses and crackles. The voice of Somersby Slim filled the room:

> I'm a travelling rep
> I go from town to town
> Some weeks sales are up
> Some weeks sales are down.
>
> Had a woman in Horncastle
> And a woman in Louth
> Loved one for her legs
> And one for her mouth.
>
> I'm a travelling rep
> Blown all over the place
> I travel with a smile
> And a heavy case.

There was Rosa in Rasen
And Sue from Scunny
Both real nice
But both after my money.

Those Brassica girls drive me wild
They leave the rest behind
Those Gainsborough girls are crazy
They always blow my mind.

I'm a travelling rep
I go from town to town
Some weeks sales are up
Some weeks sales are down.

I always get a Skeg-welcome
From the landlady at the coast,
Always ended up there,
She's the one I loved the most.

I'm a travelling man
I move from town to town
Some weeks sales are up
Some weeks sales are down.

Otis sat transfixed, his mouth open. A smile came over his face as the song faded. 'Now, that is very interesting,' he said to

Reg. 'I've never heard that song before, yet I feel I know it so well. Just listen to this.' With that, he whipped out his phone, pressed a few buttons and said, 'This is Huntsville Bubba Brown's *Travelin' Man (Tumbleweed Blues)* from Alabama in the late 1920s:

> Aint got no roots
> Got everythin' I need
> Some folks call me
> Mr Tumbleweed.
>
> When I hear the whistle
> Of the big iron train
> My itchy feet
> Start movin' again.
>
> I'm a travelin' man, seems to be my lot
> Never satisfied with what I got.
>
> I left the South
> In the back of a bus
> Just crept away
> Didn't want no fuss.

At the Windy City
I thought I'd stay
But that ol' wind
Just blew me away.

I'm a travelin' man, seems to be my lot,
Never satisfied with what I got.

One time I loved a woman
Man, you should o' seen her,
But you know me,
The grass is always greener...

I've left pretty women
Children too,
Aint proud of myself
But it's what I do.

I'm a travelin' man, seems to be my lot,
Never satisfied with what I got.

When I left the Apple
For the other side
Folks tell me
Statue of Liberty cried.

If y'ever see my tombstone
It'll be hard to read
Cos these words are carved
On tumbleweed.

I'm a travelin' man, seems to be my lot,
Never, ever satisfied with what I got.

At the finish, Reg said, trying to be polite, 'I think I know what you mean, there are certainly some similarities there.'

Otis said, 'It's remarkable! Similar structure, similar theme and yet thousands of miles apart! I'll have the team transcribe these songs and we can then engage in some deeper contextual analysis.'

Reg, who was feeling a little out of his comfort zone, said with relief, 'Ah, here's someone I think you should meet...'

As Otis was introduced to Ted, the current manager or "curator" as he liked to call himself, he was sure he saw Rob Lowe, the Hollywood actor, walk into the backroom. Ted offered to take Otis to talk to some of the old-timers – customers who had literally seen it all.

After Otis had dug into his research grant and bought a round, the conversation soon flowed. "Priming the pump" was what Otis called this technique, and it usually bore results.

Otis learned that Cultural Mick's was the first, and maybe the only, bar to retain an in-house dentist on music nights. John McCavity – known to everyone in Boston as Phil

McCavity (it's a dental joke) – used to drink there, and one night he got an urgent call from Mick to bring his little black bag in quick as Jimi Hendrix had got a little over-excited and had an accident playing the guitar with his teeth. Phil removed two teeth, a plectrum, and a G-string from Jimi's mouth. It had clearly been quite a night.

Jimi survived the ordeal and gave the teeth to Phil as a souvenir. Phil added them to his famous collection; a collection that really came on when he became Shane McGowan's dentist in the '80s. Ted proudly showed Otis his collection of musical teeth framed over the bar.

Otis noticed an old-style wanted poster on the wall next to the teeth. *Wanted: Oliver Double for crimes against comedy*.

Otis said, 'What's that all about?'

'Oh, that related to a stand-up comedy night,' said Ted. 'And what's more, that poster is displayed in every Cultural Mick's around the world.'

Otis thought he had said "stand out night", so he was keen to hear more.

Ted continued. 'That's the joker who ripped us off big-time.'

'How come?' said Otis.

'Well, every act has to fill in a contract and we all sign it – standard practice in the business. Well, this joker filled it in wrong and put his name, Double, in the space where it says "fee". Ended up getting paid twice – and he seemed such a nice guy for such a tall person. Could have been a simple mistake, but who knows? He could have pulled that stunt all over the place. Came all the way from Lincoln. You've got to watch those big city boys like a hawk. Strange, he was, couldn't keep still, bit of a punk, like a one-man mosh pit, he was. To be fair though, he was being pelted with a wide range of seasonal veg at the time.'

Otis asked Ted about Mick, the founder of the pub.

'He loved music and bringing people together; a natural in the hospitality trade. A real "man of the world" to quote Peter Green, who incidentally was never the same again after a night on the Bateman's. Everyone loved Mick and Mick loved everyone back. It was no surprise that Boston couldn't keep him long. Mick was always on the lookout for new ideas. He'd seen those Hard Rock Cafés and he realised that Cultural Mick's had international, even global, appeal. And so it proved. He was a larger-than-life character. He started many other businesses. (The Cultural brand was very flexible.) He started his own airline, his own train company, even has his own Caribbean island, Brassnecker, named in homage to himself of course and the region that gave him such a great start in life.

'Mick gave a great boost to the cabbage industry here in Brassica. He was always saying, "It's not rocket science, it's cabbage. Serve it up in tasty ways and people will lap it up". And they did, by the bucket-load.

'Mick was always fascinated by space. After all, there's a lot of it around these parts. One day, he had what he called a real "light-bulb" moment. After holding forth about the benefits of cabbage one lunchtime, he came out with the genius saying: "It's not rocket science, it's rocket fuel"! Sheer genius. In his quest for space exploration, he'd hit on the ultimate green energy source: wind power. By combining sprouts and cabbage in a secret, unique formulation and concentrating the gas into large rocket boosters, he had an almost endless supply of green power. Vegan fuel he could see, would be a real game-changer. Now, Mick controls most of the world-wide brassica cultivation and, what's more, he's already made his own first flight into space.'

'Spam fritters and junior cabbage!' someone shouted across the bar.

At first, Otis thought it was a local Country and Western act, till he realised that the food service had started.

Otis asked whether Mick ever returned to Boston, now he was acting on an intergalactic stage. Ted said he did show his face, occasionally, but like all those media figures with such high facial recognition, he tended to arrive unannounced.

Otis was getting a sense of how vibrant the Lincolnshire music scene had been. Evidently, acts from the north of the county came to the southlands on a regular basis. Ted said his favourites had always been Brigg Bill Broonzy, Leadenham Belly and, of course, the local hero, Blind Boston Stump.

Others held a candle for Big Donna Nook, who used to sing with Seal's band. Martin and Justin Timberland were also firm favourites, though they tended to play the big hotels near Woodhall Ska.

Phil joined the conversation saying he always enjoyed seeing Witham Willie Dixon, who played his own style of Witham 'n' Blues. Phil said that Dixon Street in Lincoln is named in his honour. He also liked Champion Jack Digby, T-Bone Walesby, and Scunny Boy Williamson.

When Otis let slip that courtesy of Mr English's Gainsborough archive he had actually heard some of these acts, he was urged to come back and do a kind of DJ set to bring back the old times. Otis felt a little uncomfortable as a) he wasn't really a public performer, and b) the tapes would have to be digitised and he wasn't sure how long that would take.

'You don't need to do that,' a voice piped up from the back of the room. 'You just need to get Simply Dead together again.'

The pub went quiet. Otis could sense a change in atmosphere and a chill moved across the room. 'Simply Dead?' said Otis.

'Don't listen to him,' said Ted. 'He doesn't know what he's talking about.'

'Oh yes, I do. Worked with 'em for years.'

'Actually,' said Ted, 'that is an amazing idea, but I'm not sure they'd do it. They've been retired for years, now.'

'Well, who are they?' asked Otis.

'Well, little is known about them, if truth be told, but they were evidently legendary musicians and whenever anyone of any stature on the Lincolnshire music scene passed away, they always played at the wake. No one else ever got a look in.'

Otis said, 'So they were a kind of tribute act?'

'Oh no, no, no! That's not right at all. Tribute acts imitate or copy popular acts to make money for themselves. Like that Austrian Pink Floyd act. Great laser show and alpenhorn solos, but it's not the same. No one can yodel like Dave Gilmour. No, tribute acts are a bit like parasites living off the talent of others. Simply Dead have principles and, most of all, respect for those whose music they played.'

'Why the strange name?' said Otis.

'Well, they only ever got together and play music for people who have died – they only play wakes and funeral parties. Some people think they work for the Co-op funeral service and they get advanced information about upcoming services. This gives them a chance to get on top of the music ready for the wake. But nobody really knows. But they are incredible musicians.

'Several bands who played the Gliderdrome, only really came to Mick's to try to catch some of their rare performances. Mick's used to be a popular place for wakes in times past. It's believed that Hendrix only played the guitar left-handed and upside down because the guitarist in Simply Dead played that way.'

Reg and Toby Carvery recalled that the great send-off they'd given to Screaming Jay Hykeham sent shivers down every spine in the room.

'I'm going hot and cold just remembering it now,' said Toby.

Reg reminisced about the time that the great country pickers, Foss Dyke and Torksey Lock, died in that boating accident. He said, 'Simply Dead's playing had people crying for days afterwards. Thought it could have been because the wake was held in the onion store on Arden's farm. I wonder what will happen when one of them dies. Will they mark the event, or will they just really be Simply Dead?'

They had a surprisingly good lunch, having been persuaded to push the boat out and go for the Brassica sharing platters with Brussels sprouts six ways. Otis felt it was time to get back to the office and record some of the day's rich pickings. However, it was clear that he would have to return to Boston as there was still so much to see and experience, not least going further south into the fabled Vinyl Triangle,

On his way out, after standing next to a guy in the gents who looked exactly like Rob Lowe, Otis caught the eye of the character who had first mentioned Simply Dead. With a flick of his head, he gestured that they should meet outside.

Otis said, 'That was very interesting what you told us in there. What else do you know about Simply Dead?'

There was a pause, and Otis opened his wallet to again tap into the research grant. A crisp twenty quid changed hands and Otis could see that he'd done the right thing.

'It's a start, but it'll cost you more than twenty sobs, old son!'

Otis peeled off two more, and the man started talking. Otis silently pressed his Dictaphone in his jacket pocket and said,

'And who exactly am I speaking to?'

'Jack Sabbath's the name, and I was their roadie. I used to drive the hearse that they carried their gear in. I also kept the diary of every wake they ever played – dates, times, set lists, everything.'

Otis gulped, 'This is very interesting,' in a way that utterly failed to disguise his excitement.

'It'll cost you...'

Otis thought of his fast dwindling research grant. He could see the amount that he had husbanded so well disappearing fast. *But that's what it's for*, he told himself reassuringly. 'I'm sure we can come to some agreement that suits us both.'

After swapping phone numbers, they went their separate ways.

Otis turned and shouted, 'What's your name again?'

'Jack Sabbath, but folks round here call me Old Bolingbroke!'

Otis fished out one of his cards, the type that American academics use to impress people with at conferences.

'Dr Otis K. Spanner III, Professor of Comparative Anthropology (Music and Popular Culture).'

Old Bolingbroke took one look at it, and said to himself, *Bloody hell, don't tell there are two other Spanners walking this earth.*

CHAPTER 6

Brassica, the Vinyl Triangle and the Deep South

Otis drove down to Boston again, and met up with Reg Carvery. Reg had offered to take Otis on a tour of the southland, into deep bulb and cabbage country.

Otis was hoping to visit some of the record stores he'd been hearing so much about in the so-called "Vinyl Triangle". Uptown Vinyl, for some reason, was located in a garden centre on the edge of Spalding, the tulip bulb capital of England. Also, he'd heard great things about a wise old dealer, the mysterious "Bob" who ran an independent record shop just over the fenland border in Whittlesey. In truth, at certain times of the year it wasn't even possible to see the border, as it was under water. A local lad, Ramsey Lewis, wrote a tune about the travails of life in the Fens, called *Wade in the Water*.

Reg was a great companion on the road trip. He was knowledgeable and seemed to know everyone. In fact, it turned out that he was related to most of the people they met that day. The Fens are like that – not many people move away.

Nowadays, most folks do have ten fingers and ten toes, though occasionally they still find some with webbing in between.

Otis asked Reg why nearly all the places they had travelled through were called Gedney. Reg said it was all the Germans' fault. In the late 1930s as World War Two was approaching, it was decided in the event of a German invasion, they would remove as many road signs and village names as possible, and call them all Gedney to confuse the invading forces. One night, during a Home Guard exercise, a siren had gone off and, in their enthusiasm, all the signs were duly unscrewed and dumped in The Wash. Reg said this had really buggered up the local taxi business in Boston for years. Everybody wanted to go home to Gedney, after a night out, but very few got home before the morning. Some parts of the county never recovered. As Otis looked out of the car window, he could see that settlements were indeed few and far between.

As the sun reflected off a bright surface, Otis commented on the sudden large areas of cultivation under glass. Reg, a veg man through and through, grimaced and said, 'Ah yes, the flower industry.' It was clear from his sneer that the only flowers he rated were cauliflowers.

'Ah, The Smiths have a lot to answer for,' said Reg. 'When that Morrissey, their front man, started going on stage with bunches of gladioli in his pockets, the business boomed. Overnight, whole fields of cabbages were grubbed up and turned over to the cultivation of multi-coloured flowers. They couldn't grow 'em and cut 'em fast enough.'

Johnny Marr, Otis had read somewhere, had said that The Smiths would have made twice as much money from their relatively short career if it hadn't been for Morrissey's gladioli habit.

Reg said that when The Smiths broke up, whole businesses went bust overnight, and it was only a concerted effort to get Elton John to buy British that got the industry back on its feet.

As they travelled further south, and the sun got marginally hotter, Reg said, 'Did you notice that last sign? We're now in the South Holland district of Brassica.'

Otis was confused. As far as he knew, Brassica was not connected to mainland Europe, even at particularly low tides.

Reg said, 'Europe's been coming to Lincolnshire for centuries! Indeed, these vast, wet flatlands were known to the early Roman invaders as the kingdom of Brassica on account of the cabbage, sprouts and kale they found here. They then introduced their own exotic varieties like broccoli, calabrese and Savoy cabbage. Holland is a reference to the Dutch who were drafted in as drainage experts to drain the Fens and create the fertile land we see today.'

Otis found all this fascinating, and he took a deep breath and filled his lungs with the slightly sulphurous aroma that permeated everything there.

Having mentioned the war a little earlier, Reg came back to the topic as they passed the site of an old World War Two airfield. 'You know that another name for Lincolnshire is Bomber County?'

Otis said he'd heard the term, but didn't know much about it. This was music to Reg's ears. His second favourite thing in life, after veg of course, was talking about the RAF and its Lincolnshire connections.

In truth, Otis would have been more at home talking about REM, but sitting captive in Reg's 4x4 he had no choice but to feign interest.

Reg started by saying that the government had always taken a special interest in Lincolnshire, and it still did today. To Otis, this sounded slightly sinister, but he let Reg continue his story.

Reg said that at the start of the war, the Air Ministry had called a meeting with the major farmers in Brassica and had wanted them to join together in secret research to support the war effort.

A man called Barnes Wallis led the project. It was a little known fact said Reg because obviously it was classified information at the time, that the first bouncing bomb prototypes were actually Lincolnshire cabbages. It was a marriage made in Heaven, said Reg.

'We could grow the ammunition, we had the airfields, and the Lancaster bombers to drop them. Who'd have thought that Brassica's contribution to modern warfare was so significant?'

At one point, when munitions factories were under attack, a plan had been hatched to simply drop a particularly hard type of cabbage directly onto German targets.

In a highly secretive collaboration between the Air Ministry and the Ministry of Food, many square miles of weapons-grade cabbages were farmed in the war years. What more terrifying killing machine could there be – a huge Lancaster bomber loaded to the gunnels with its prime, lethal cargo? (Well, lethal when dropped from thirty-two thousand feet.)

Reg pointed over towards Gedney Dyke and said that just over there was a very top-secret lab, where they had developed different coloured cabbages. They had been looking for a strain that would evade radar detection. The project failed, leaving only two options – the green and red varieties – but both showed up on the radar, so the default fallback position was to eat the stuff.

In the end, more red cabbages were dropped on German targets, as it was found that the unexploded green ones were being recycled into sauerkraut. Given that we were on rations here, it didn't seem right to be helping the enemy out by express delivery of its favourite food. So, red it was.

Reg then stunned Otis by saying that many of the government research facilities still existed today.

'Look over there', said Reg pointing towards Gedney Drove End. 'See that?'

Otis screwed his eyes up and could see what looked like acre upon acre of glass houses that appeared to be full of flowers. 'What, those glasshouses?'

Reg smiled and said, 'That's what you think you are seeing, but in actual fact that's one of the government's top-secret stealth facilities. The only glasshouses growing flowers are on the perimeter, but everything else, well, even I'm not sure what goes on in there, deep in the interior.'

Otis was astounded by the sheer scale of the operation. As they travelled towards Gedney St Peters, there was another large expanse of glass.

'Another government facility?' asked Otis.

'Ah no, that one's now in private hands. Actually, Mick's Cultural Organisation bought that after hearing about developments in the textile industry.'

Otis, having grown up in the Cotton Belt in the deep South, thought he knew a bit about textiles. He'd always thought how clever it was that someone had seen this shrub growing and had had the vision to turn it into all sorts of apparel. What kind of guy looks at a field of plants and sees them as row upon row of socks, sweatshirts, and underpants? Genius – sheer genius!

Reg picked up on this thought and said there was a history of entrepreneurs making clothing from natural things. As well as cotton he'd heard of people making clothes out of bamboo. Hell, even the Wellington boots that helped open up the Fens to human habitation had grown on rubber trees in Malaya, he'd been reliably informed.

'We have the Irish to thank for the next giant leap in textile technology,' said Reg. 'A Mr Arthur Ryan.'

'Ah,' said Otis, 'the owner of Ryanwear?'

'The very same,' said Reg. 'He developed a process for making clothing out of potatoes; started a business called Primark, and became massively successful over in Ireland. A

British company – Associated British Foods – bought him out and helped finance expansion in the UK. They now have a landmark store in London's Oxford Street, and it's at the posh end too, near Marble Arch. And every item of clothing, allegedly, made from potatoes! What a story!'

'So, what's that huge complex over there?' asked Otis.

'That is Cultural Mick's answer to Ryanwear. It's a cabbage textile plant. The biggest in the world. Cabbage produces much finer and stronger fabric than potatoes.'

Otis marvelled at the versatility of this wonder crop.

Reg said to Otis, 'Have you ever grown cabbages yourself?' as if it was something that everybody indulged in.

'Er, no, can't say I've ever tried to be honest,' Otis had to admit, and on saying that, Reg put the brakes on hard and stopped at the side of the road.

'Get out. I want to show you something.'

Otis got out. Reg had a can of Cultural Mick's cauliflower cordial Cola and he poured it over a cabbage.

'See that?' shouted Reg. 'See how the liquid forms tiny silver balls and runs off the plant? The R&D people realised that the leaves of most brassicas repel liquid. This stuff is naturally waterproof. And that's why the Cultural Organisation is the biggest producer of waterproof outerwear in the world. It was discovered that the outer leaves of red cabbages were the best of all and this was reserved for the top-of-the-range fashion brands. It's like the cashmere of cabbages.' Reg said that a high street shop called Monsoon evidently used to sell a lot of Lincolnshire rainwear.

Reg, clearly proud of this local ingenuity and business acumen, talked about other success stories that had grown up on the back of the thriving cabbage textile industry. The trick, Reg explained, was to give people what they needed *and* what they wanted.

'Take windows, for example.'

'You make windows out of cabbages?' Otis spluttered. 'You've got to be joking, Reg.'

Reg carried on. 'Every house has windows, OK?'

'Yes,' said Otis, 'I'll grant you that, but—'

'And windows need curtains or blinds.'

'True,' said Otis.

'The superior insulation qualities of the Brassica textile range were an ideal fit!' said Reg triumphantly. 'Cabbage Inc. set up two businesses to cover the market: Curtain Lindsey to the north and The Blind Boys of Brassica in the south. Covered the whole county, exclusively using home-grown material.'

'Sheer genius,' said Otis, who was a big fan of The Blind Boys of Alabama, never knowing that they had a Lincolnshire counterpart.

Reg, always keen to talk about the many Lincolnshire entrepreneurial success stories, waxed lyrical about another branch of the company. 'It's Curtains for You – purveyors of drapery and small curtains for the crematorium trade. Damned near got a monopoly of that market, now.'

This reminded Reg of another local businessman's idea to

open a chain of refreshment bars or cafés at crematoriums; the thinking being that people often arrived early, and instead of standing about, it might have been helpful to have somewhere to get a drink and pass the time. The "Café Crem" concept was turned down on grounds of bad taste. Reg said he thought they needed to get the blend and roast right before trying again.

Pretty soon they arrived at Spalding, and found their way to Uptown Vinyl.

Bit of a strange set-up, thought Otis, wondering why and how a Kirkcudbright lifeboat had ended up high and dry near the entrance to a garden centre, many miles from the sea. For goodness' sake, Kirkcudbright was somewhere in Scotland, about two hundred and eighty miles away. There was also a kids' playground, a café, and what seemed like acre upon acre of plastic and cement garden ornaments. Oh, and a pet shop with an exotic creatures' section. Somewhere, in among all that, was a record shop.

There seemed a lot of slightly bemused elderly people, clearly out for the day. By the looks of some, they were out of it, full stop. Many seemed to have gravitated to the café that sold an extraordinary range of fillings for the jacket potatoes that most seemed to have come for. Some of them had clearly been to Uptown Vinyl, judging by the way they clutched their precious carrier bags. Otis had noticed that all good record shops had distinctive carrier bags tastefully advertising themselves, and Uptown Vinyl was no exception. As Otis surveyed some of the smiling vacant faces, he wondered whether some of the older customers ever got confused. He mentioned this to Reg, who said he'd heard reports that one old boy had gone looking for a Whitesnake album, but had gone into the pet shop by mistake, and went home with a six-foot albino python. Reg said the boys at Uptown Vinyl had said that the albino ones were quite rare and, if it was in good condition, were worth a bob or two. They did say that the ones that brought most money were the ones in their original skins, but they hardly ever turn up, a bit like that Beatles albino album – the low numbers never turned up, but they must be out there somewhere.

Uptown Vinyl had walls covered with highly collectable album artwork memorabilia. Otis's eyes lingered, perhaps a little too long, on the Hendrix *Electric Ladyland* cover. (It certainly didn't have those ladies on the US version.)

The guy behind the counter saw all this and said to Otis, 'Hendrix played here, you know.'

'What, here at the garden centre?'

'No, here in Spalding', and he rummaged around to find an old handbill for the gig.

Otis had to sit down. He'd never seen a line-up like this one. This out-Montereyed Monterey; it quite possibly out-Woodstocked Woodstock!

'The Jimi Hendrix Experience, Cream, Pink Floyd, the Move, Geno Washington and his Ram Jam Band, and Zoot Money and his Big Roll Band – all for one pound!'

The poster promised "a knockout atmosphere", "soft

ultraviolet lights" and "hot dogs". *You couldn't even get a miniature toy hot dog today for a pound*, thought Otis. Evidently, on the strength of offering the "exotic" American hot dogs on the bill, the concert was called Barbeque '67, and was held in the Spalding Tulip Bulb Auction Hall.

So, it was held in a kind of garden centre, after all, thought Otis.

He did a quick calculation and worked out that this was only eighteen days before the fabled Monterey festival in California that turned Hendrix into a global guitar god.

Again, thought Otis, *Lincolnshire is right on the money.*

All this talking of hot dogs made Otis feel hungry. After a quick curried cabbage pasty, it was on the road again. Before setting out, Otis tried to find a restroom via rooms full of soft toys, plastic flowers, and the most revolting novelties and gifts that no one in their right minds would ever want in their home. Well, that's how Otis felt, but people seemed to be buying stuff as if it were going out of fashion. When he returned, Reg was on his phone.

Reg said that as a special treat he'd just fixed it to take Otis around one of the very latest top-secret Cultural Mick's R&D labs. Otis would have to sign a confidentiality agreement before being granted access.

What looked like a cabbage processing plant turned out to be the most hi-tech environment imaginable. The level of security was so high that it took a good half hour to proceed about five yards. The duty manager conveyed Reg and Otis on the internal mag-lev system, to the director's office at the heart of the complex. Everyone wore crisp white overalls except the director, Ms Gina Broccoli, who wore a white scientist's coat over a black suit. She also sported large black matching glasses that reminded Otis of Brains, the resident genius in *Thunderbirds*. After offering cabbage smoothies, she gave Otis a brief history of the company.

She said it all started a long time ago when a Lincolnshire lad, Zak Newton, had a cabbage fall on his head. When this had happened, he discovered two things: gravity and concussion. Zak's story had appealed to a US airman stationed in Brassica during World War Two, and when he returned to California after the war, he took the idea but changed the cabbage to an apple. Apple has now become one of the biggest companies in the world. It was Mick's idea to reclaim Zak Newton's legacy and, therefore, he set up his own media company called Cabbage. This is now the parent company of the Cultural Mick's Organisation. A bit like Alphabet and Google, she explained – most people have heard of Google, but very few of Alphabet.

She said nothing pleases Mick more then to see experts on TV with their laptops open, revealing the distinctive cabbage logo with the tiny bite out of its right side.

'So, what's special about this place?' she asked rhetorically.

She then went on to answer her own question, telling them that this very building was the nerve centre of the Cabbage media operation. Cabbage stalk fibres were produced for use around the globe. In fact, enough produced each day to go around the globe several times. Those were twenty times better for conveying data than flimsy fibre optic cable and, importantly, much cheaper to produce.

After the initial success of the Cultural Mick's pubs, the business had developed into one of the greatest global media undertakings, and most of it built on Brassica-produced cabbage.

Before embarking on a tour of the complex, she outlined some of the other exciting ventures in the pipeline: a possible tie-up with Danish company Lego to produce bricks made of a cabbage composite material. Current world production stood at thirty-six billion bricks a year – that's one hundred and twenty-five million every day – all made of plastic, with a significant carbon footprint. 'Our cabbage composite bricks can reduce that dramatically.' Things were at an advanced stage of negotiation, so she couldn't say more.

'As we are such a large media player, we are always in need of content. We tried a tie-up with Disney, but they weren't willing to play ball. A pity really, given they have serious links with Lincs.'

'What do you mean?' said Otis. To his mind, nothing could be more American than Disney, and all its works.

'Oh, didn't you know? Walt's family originated in Lincolnshire – a village just outside Lincoln, on the way to Newark – Norton Disney. Walt even visited once, and there used to be a picture of him holding a pint of beer in the village pub The Vincent Arms.'

'You're kidding me?' said Otis.

'No, it's the gospel truth!' Ms Broccoli said. 'Evidently, his family came over with William the Conqueror and the Normans in 1066. Original family name was d'Isigny, meaning from the village of Isigny-sur-Mer, in Normandy.'

Otis was a little shell-shocked. 'First you tell me Walt had family in Lincolnshire, then you hit me with the fact that he came from France! What next?'

'That's it,' said Ms Broccoli. 'Anyway, the Disney Corporation didn't want to join us, though they were open to using some of our locations and studios for some of their *Star Wars* movies. Again, it's very hush-hush. We have developed on this site a state-of-the-art suite of film and TV studios. Indeed, a member of my own family, Uncle Cubby, was asking about making the next James Bond movie, *From Brassica with Love*, here. But again, Professor Spanner, I must insist that you keep this under your hat!

'To be honest,' continued Ms Broccoli, 'we would rather concentrate on developing our own in-house home-grown products. We have great hopes for a show our scouts discovered somewhere near Washingborough. We think it could be really, really big. Bigger than *Friends*. It's a show with universal appeal that reaches into every home.'

Gina, as she insisted on being called, pressed a few buttons, and spoke to a rather robotic voice somewhere else in the building.

She turned to Otis and said, 'If you can come back later in the week – let's say, Friday – you can sit in on a production meeting for our new show, and maybe stay on for a recording of a pilot, later in the day.'

Otis felt this was an offer he couldn't refuse, especially since it came from someone so powerful (and with an Italian surname to boot). Reg took Otis back to Boston, where he picked up his own car for the now familiar drive to Lincoln.

Otis had not expected his day to turn out like this. *Who knew about Lincolnshire's own Brassica Valley?* Otis thought to himself. *Such innovation and enterprise, and all under the radar!*

It looked as if the trip to Bob's Records in Whittlesey would have to wait for another day.

CHAPTER 7

Radio Brassica and Some Office Work

On the drive back to the university, Otis received a phone call from one of his research assistants, Mary. She was covering the Lincoln area and had contacted the local radio station in order to try to locate people who had been in the audience when The Beatles had played at the ABC Cinema on Thursday twenty-eighth November 1963.

Mary said the station had loved it; there was nothing better they liked to do than reach out and ask the public to get in touch. Evidently, it ticked some "community engagement" box, her source had said. Also, they were keen to invite Otis into the studio so that he could talk, at length, about his fieldwork and findings. Before hanging up, she said they'd been inundated with calls – so far about five thousand people were claiming to have been at the concert – a venue that had a capacity just under two thousand! This set Otis thinking that the team would have to devise a series of questions to sift out those who only wished they had been there from those who had actually attended. He'd get Mary on to that as soon as possible.

Otis switched on the car radio and turned to Radio Brassica. It was the *Daphne Heckington Show* – aka the Queen of the Cabbage Patch. It took a while to tune in to the conversation.

Daphne kept listing words that meant nothing to Otis: Aldi, Nisa, Lidl, Spar, Co-op, Asda...

Local Brassica terms, he wondered. *New varieties of potatoes, perhaps?*

Daphne ploughed on. 'What have all these in common?'

After several fruitless guesses, one Doris from Belchford said that the other day she'd been to visit her sister in Lincoln and she was pretty sure that they were all supermarkets.

'Bingo!' shouted Daphne. 'Now we're cooking on cabbage gas! But there's one other thing that links them all. Can you see it?'

Otis thought that given this was radio that was a bit of an unfair question, but after another twenty minutes of wild stabs in the dark, Edith Spouge, a keen Scrabble player from Goltho, said that she'd spotted that they were all four-letter words.

'Brassica bingo – jackpot!' exploded Daphne. 'So, my question to you is...' and Otis could almost sense her moving closer to the microphone for the big reveal, 'my question to you: should Tesco shorten its name? Is it losing out to its shorter-named competitors? Should it be Esco or Tesc? Give us a call – we'd love to hear your views!'

The next two hours were crazy, not that the journey took two hours, but on arrival at the university car park he couldn't leave the car. This was radio on another level.

Ken, from Gedney All Saints, said he was a regular Waitrose shopper, but he could see why those other places were cheaper. He pointed out that with a shorter name they could save on printing costs, advertising, carrier bags – everything.

'If they can slash costs there, they can cut corners everywhere,' he said. 'It gives them a big advantage.'

Ken suggested Waitrose got in on the act and ditched its first and last two letters to call itself Itro. He also said Tesco should definitely go with Esco.

Norma from Normanby (no relation) called in quite upset, saying she felt sorry for Poundstretcher. With a name that long, they were seriously behind the competition. She said surely something should be done. Otis could visualise Daphne nodding along in the studio. He also anticipated her now almost automatic response.

'Well, what do you think? Give us a call, we'd love to hear your views! '

Daphne could sense that this topic was running out of steam, probably because her producer in the control booth had opened his mouth wide and was making exaggerated yawning gestures with his right hand. So, she quickly wound up that part of the show by saying she'd be in touch with Tesco's head office and would inform them of this morning's survey. Most listeners favoured renaming Tesco Esco, and she said she'd try to have an interview with the Tesco CEO on tomorrow's show.

At the end of the *Daphne Heckington Show*, Otis felt like he needed a shower, so he couldn't begin to think what she felt like. He was just about to switch off when he was startled by a loud siren. He looked around, only to realise that it was actually on the radio and was a trailer for the next show, *Sprain or Strain?*

An authoritative deep male voice urgently barked over the siren: 'Will the ambulance be racing to your house today? Sprain or strain? Phone in and tell us your symptoms, and let our studio doctor give you a free, on-air diagnosis! Could you be our blue light special today? Stay on the line to find out! Remember, together with the expertise of our on-air doctor, and votes from you, our wonderful listeners, one of you out there will be waiting in A&E tonight! *Sprain or Strain?* coming up next!'

As Otis walked towards his office, he could feel a headache coming on.

Back in the office, Otis read an email from the Head of School inviting him to the next school review board meeting. He had been invited to explain the progress made so far on his research project to a team of SADs – Senior Academic Directors. Now that progress was going so well, Otis could actually look forward to sharing his work with, what he hopedthe, were his supportive colleagues.

Not having attended such a meeting there before, he decided to have an informal chat with Neil Middleton, one of the SADs in his own college, just to learn a few ground rules, etcetera.

Arriving a few minutes early, he found Dr Middleton sitting on his assistant's desk making sure that their respective diaries were up to date and in sync.

Neil said, 'Come through,' and he waved Otis into his rather minimalist and sparsely furnished office.

Otis couldn't help noticing how remarkably tidy and clear of paper the desk was.

'Wow, great view!' said Otis.

Neil said, 'All the best offices here look up towards the cathedral, which reminds me, I must go in there sometime. Now, Otis, how's it going? Well, I hope?'

Otis replied positively and said he was keen to share his findings with a wider group.

'Good. Let me give you some advice,' said Neil. 'Keep it short, bullet points, less is more. You can always expand, in the unlikely event that someone asks you a question.'

'Oh,' said Otis. 'If that's how it's done, that will certainly save me and my team some work.'

'Ah yes,' said Neil. 'Your team...'

Otis said, 'Great bunch of people, those PhD student-researchers. They really work hard.'

'Glad to hear,' Neil said. 'But I'm afraid the Head of School has asked me to inform you that we're going to have to take two of them off you to fulfil some undergraduate teaching commitments.'

'But my funding is covering those research assistants, and we have a great many findings to analyse and process.'

'I know, I know, I don't doubt that for a second, old chap, but I'm sure you'll be able to cope with this, er, new situation.'

'Neil, I really need those people. We have so much work still to do.'

'I do hope you don't propose to make too much of a fuss about this, Otis. These things happen all the time. We all have to get used to it these days.'

Otis asked Neil about his own work. What, for instance, did he actually teach? Neil visibly blanched and said of course he'd like to teach more, but the current demands of his job made that very difficult.

'So, what exactly is it that you do?' asked Otis.

Neil took a deep breath as he tried to think how best to explain what his post entailed. 'In a nutshell, my job is to ensure that the university meets its targets and recruits enough students to its courses. When I say the university meets its targets, I mean the individual colleges, schools, departments – they are the ones who have targets to meet. If targets are met then everybody's happy, and I get a bonus.'

Otis said, 'And if targets are not met, for some particular reason?'

'Well, should the courses not reach their targets, then it's part of my job to help sort this in more creative ways, for example, get rid of surplus staff in order to balance the books. If I can hit the target that way then again, I get a bonus. It's all part of a mysterious economic cycle.'

'So,' Otis said, 'let me see if I've got this correct. If the courses are full, you have done a good job, but if the courses have vacancies, then they are at fault?'

'Exactly!' smiled Neil.

'So how,' asked Otis, warming to his task, 'do you know which part of the economic cycle you are in at any given time?'

'Erm, well... Well, of course, that's the difficult thing. We never really actually know because the situation is so fluid...'

'So, you don't actually know which strategy to deploy at any given time, is that what you're really saying?'

'I suppose it could be interpreted in that way, but I do feel that you don't really understand some of the particular challenges we face in HE in the UK,' said Neil. 'That's why the job is so difficult, er, challenging, but we always have the PT option.'

'PT option? What's that?' said Otis.

'Ah, the PT option: if in doubt, get rid of the part-timers. And, if numbers are up next academic year, then they are always grateful to be re-engaged.'

'But let me get this straight,' said Otis, who was a very straight-thinking kind of guy. 'If you have part-timers, aren't you employing them because you need their skills and talents to actually make the timetable work?'

'Ah,' said Neil, 'it's not quite as simple as that where budgets and targets are concerned.'

Or bonuses, thought Otis, but he managed to bite his tongue.

Neil said that it had been good to get together like this, must do it more often. He also said, 'Don't put too much work into the forthcoming meeting as the Head of School has a dreadful habit of cancelling them at the last minute.' He asked Otis if he had heard the rumour that the VC was in the running for another job. He said he'd love to be a fly on the wall and read the VC's CV.

As they walked out of the faculty building, Otis raised again the topic of his research assistants. Neil, not at all wishing to re-open that can of worms, rapidly said his goodbyes, walking backwards, with one arm raised, partly in acknowledgment, and partly defensive, inevitably to the accompaniment of, 'I'll get back to you on that one.' This usually being his last word on any subject.

Later that night when wading through his emails – so many, and so many of little or no relevance to him whatsoever – he noticed a copy of the school's monthly newsletter. He noted a picture of himself and the Head of School welcoming him to his year at Lindum. It also said he was an expert on Gainsborough.

Ah, he thought, *that's where the VC got the wrong end of the stick. Art historians, they think there's no other kind...*

Another email explained that the minister had "called in" the Tate gallery idea for further consultation.

Otis settled down to finalise details for tomorrow's trip to Market Rasen.

CHAPTER 8

On to Market Rasen and Horncastle

After meeting Mr English in Gainsborough, Otis had many more leads and contacts to follow up. He had already been handed cuttings from the *Grimsby Telegraph*, dealing with local music legends Bernie Taupin and Rod Temperton.

Stopping off at Market Rasen, Otis soon found people willing to talk about Bernie. In the veg shop by the small square he learned about the day Elton John had come to town. This was in 1971, when Bernie had married his first wife in the local Catholic Church, where he had once been an altar boy. Elton had been the best man, of course, and they had both stayed the night before the wedding at the local Limes Hotel. The next day Elton, the artist formerly known as Reg, signed the church marriage register with his real name, Reginald Dwight

Otis was told to visit the Aston Arms pub, and in the corner he met a wizened old boy who said he used to play pool with Bernie in this very pub over half a century ago (and Bernie still owed him half a crown).

After buying Ron a drink, he began to open up about the old days. Otis switched his Dictaphone on.

Ron had many memories, and said he had followed Bernie and Elton's careers avidly. He did keep mentioning that half-crown, but it was probably water under the bridge now.

He told Otis that Bernie's real name was Bernard Tarpaulin, and he was evidently a very talented piano player, and Reg, who could be quite waspish, was very good with words. So, they teamed up and started writing songs.

Management soon stepped in and said that nobody was going to make it with a name like Tarpaulin, unless, of course, they were a covers band. So, reluctantly, Bernie agreed to a name change. At first, he became Bernie Tie-pin. (Being the piano player, he always wore a flamboyant tie-pin to stop his large kipper ties falling over the keyboard.) Eventually there was a compromise, and he became Bernie Taupin.

Reg, feeling a bit miffed after paying for extra piano lessons, had a bit of a hissy fit and demanded a name change too. He said he was now a better piano player, and he would only carry on if he could tinkle the ivories and call himself Mavis Enderby. (Now, all true yellow-bellies will know that this is the name of a lovely village in the Lincolnshire Wolds much loved by all those who visit Tennyson country). Management didn't know, didn't care and, to be honest, didn't think Mavis was going to cut it. Eventually, Reg settled on a safer name that he still used today. It was said that he coined the name from two musicians he'd met on the London scene: Elton Dean the sax player, and

Long John Baldy, the white blues singer. So he might have been Dean Long (let's face it, nobody would actually pick Baldy as a name, though Elton later flirted with this, until he had a successful hair transplant. And lovely it looks too! What a man, and what a mane!) So, it was welcome to Elton, and farewell to the artist formerly known as Reg.

After this Ron clammed up until Otis bought him another pint of Old Codswallop, a local Grimsby real ale.

Otis learned that having been born near Sleaford, Bernie had lived in the village of Owmby-by-Spital, near Rasen (as the locals called it).

Early in 1970, Bernie and Elton collaborated on an album called *Tumbleweed Connection*. This album was considered a "concept" album in that the songs were Country and Western in flavour and were usually catalogued as Americana. But clearly the songs were rooted in wildest Lincolnshire, and Bernie's own local country background shines through. It is rumoured that the album was originally entitled *Rasen Hell*, a concept album about a wild frontier town in deepest Lincolnshire. There are many clues to support this theory. Indeed, the choice of the title *Tumbleweed* evidently, according to Ron, was a local yellow-belly term for the wacky-backy that was becoming increasingly popular at the end of the '60s and early '70s, especially with the art school crowd in Lincoln, and with musicians in particular; Tumbleweed, so-called because of the effects after a few puffs of what was also called the magic dragon.

The record company really pushed for the Americana angle though, and the eventual album released contained a few changes from the original Lincolnshire masterpiece.

My Father's Gun was originally called *My Father's Gin* after Bernie's dad's favourite tipple; likewise, *Ballad of a Well-Known Gun*, also known locally as *Gordon's Song*. *Country Comfort* really summed up the joys of living the Lincolnshire life. It mentions the 6.09 a.m. train "roaring past the creek". This, of course, refers to the early train to Cleethorpes, which, Ron told Otis, also stopped at Grimsby.

The album cover again tended to fall in line with the view that this was meant to be a homage to Lincolnshire living. It was meant to look like a Wild West station – clearly, that's what the record company wanted. However, closer analysis revealed that this was in fact an English station, and its walls were covered in English adverts for a wide range of products: *The Daily Telegraph* costing one (old) penny, Stone's Original Ginger Wine, Shelvey's Mineral Waters (from Brighton), and Hudson's Super Soap to name but a few. It was Otis's hunch that this was, in fact, none other than Market Rasen station itself, and that the album far from being about American Country and Western themes, was actually dealing with homespun Lincolnshire life.

Later Otis verified (quite quickly by checking the charity shops in Rasen) that American Country and Western music had infiltrated those parts to an alarming degree; dozens of Jim Reeves, Hank Williams, and Slim Whitman albums dominating the Rasen charity shop shelves.

Not only that, Otis was amazed to discover that Market Rasen station still existed. So many places in Lincolnshire no longer seemed to have access to the railway, that it was a joy to visit such an iconic spot. Otis took many photographs to include in his final report.

Otis had spent so much time plying Ron with pints of Old Codswallop that he felt he didn't really have time to explore Great Grimsby in the few hours that remained. That would have to wait for another day. Ron suggested another one for the road.

When Otis playfully questioned what road that might be, Ron said, 'The Yellow Brick Road, of course!'

Otis bought him a whisky chaser, too. Eventually, as Ron struggled to make his way to the gents, he said how he'd enjoyed those Saturday nights fighting with the lads who came over from Caistor looking for trouble. He said Rasen was very quiet these days. Most likely, all the tearaways and teddy boys would be riddled with arthritis now, or have passed away. He said to Otis, 'If you ever see Bernie in America, remind him about my half-crown.'

After talking to Gloria, the landlady, he decided to travel on to Horncastle and see what he could learn there. The initial research hadn't thrown anything like the riches he'd uncovered in Market Rasen.

Horncastle gave the initial impression of being nothing much more than a collection of antique shops and antique people. No problem there though, as when looking at the past he'd found that young people are little help.

In a rather over-crowded second-hand bookshop (over-crowded with books, not customers) Otis found a helpful guide who turned out to be delighted to share his local knowledge.

Otis heard tell of a remarkable Lincolnshire figure, Sir Joseph Banks. In 1802 (*that's seventeen years before Alabama was even a US state*, thought Otis) Sir Joseph earned his nickname "River" Banks by straightening out and canalising the river Bain between Horncastle and the River Witham at Dogdyke. Before the coming of the railways, this connected Horncastle to the wider world. Linking the Wolds to the fertile flat lands of Brassica changed everything, and Horncastle became a busy bursting little town.

This linking of the two rivers opened up what was called at the time the Wolds Wide Web, a communications network that enabled fast deliveries by carrier pigeon, pack horse and canal boat. Today we are used to ordering stuff from our desktops, laptops or even phones, and having things delivered the very next day. We tended to think this was revolutionary and the cutting edge of modernity. Amazon had become one of the bigger companies in the world serving our need for (almost) instant gratification.

However, as the conversation progressed. Otis discovered that Lincolnshire had evolved a sophisticated system that pre-dated Amazon by at least a couple of centuries. When interviewing older Lincolnshire folk about the musical past, he kept encountering the term "Got it off Witham". This could refer to buying an instrument, new strings, or sheet music, in fact, almost anything at all.

Evidently, an enterprising shopkeeper in downtown Boston hit on the idea of using the Wolds Wide Web to set up a speedy delivery service. People would send in orders by carrier pigeon, and he would despatch the goods ASAP saying, "It'd be with 'em before you could say Jack Robinson". (Otis made a note to look up this Jack Robinson later). It was a great way to get things delivered, long before the advent of the Bezos behemoth. Once this service took off, the Lincolnshire music scene exploded. After all, what's a bass guitar without strings? Exactly – a lump of wood.

The forerunner of Amazon Prime was the" With 'em Tomorrow" service, but to be fair, said the local historian, it was only ever patchy on account of various birds of prey feasting on the flocks of pigeons criss-crossing the county skies. *That rings a bell*, thought Otis, as he remembered being told that there was a pair of green falcon breeding on top of Lincoln Cathedral to this very day.

Wow, thought Otis, *yet another case of Lincolnshire delivering again!*

On the way to Lincoln, Otis noticed signposts to Bardney. This reminded him of the Great Western Music Festival that he was beginning to hear quite a lot about. He'd start to look into that tonight.

CHAPTER 9

The Festivals They Could Not Stop!

Otis had to ask, 'Why Great Western?' when it was clear that this festival was about as far east as you could get in England.

The festival poster was dominated by an old-style American locomotive, complete with cowcatcher on the front. Otis thought that maybe the same people that wanted to turn *Tumbleweed Connection* into an American album were to blame. Looking at the line-up, it was obvious that home-grown talent outnumbered the American acts heavily.

It was Spring Bank holiday weekend, May 1972 and, as some suggested, not the most sensible time to hold a large outdoor event in England. April showers often didn't realise that there were only thirty days in April and so continued to rain down in May as well. And they did – with a vengeance. The Bardney festival was a total mud bath by the end of the weekend.

It had originally been scheduled to take place in Kent, but residents objected strongly and eventually, after wrangling in court, the festival ended up in Lincolnshire. Its organisers included the film actor Stanley Baker and he was backed (i.e. bankrolled by Lord Harlech, who was clearly hoping to make a bob or two out of the youngsters and their sudden love of listening to loud music in fields.) In the event, the festival lost about fifty thousand pounds – quite a sum in those days.

Otis's researchers had turned up a film, now available on YouTube, made by the British Film Institute that explored this new phenomenon of rock festivals. It made great viewing. One got the impression that certain well-spoken, well-dressed older people were looking to make a killing out of this fashionable new type of entertainment. They seemed pretty certain that they had the organisation and manpower to do it, too. The film showed some of the preparations, with large white fences slicing through fields cultivated with peas. They also talked of having great security in place. There certainly seemed a great number of police in the area.

The film focused on some of the locals and their natural concerns about this influx of, as a local police commander stated, "long-haired, sometimes dirty people, gathered around in very large numbers".

The festival only went ahead after the High Court had imposed an injunction on three points: congestion of roads, trespassing, and noise. John Martin, the event's chief booker stated: "If any of these occur, we face a maximum prison sentence of six months". Fortunately, Lord Harlech and his chums didn't have to do "time" in Lincoln Prison.

It cost £4.50 for a weekend ticket and, like the recent Isle of Wight Festival, was spread over four days instead of the more usual three. The organisers had chosen, as a nice Lincolnshire touch, Booming Bob Harris to compère the event. Bob's relative, "Bomber" Harris was, of course, partly responsible for the county's alternative name of "Bomber County". By a happy coincidence, Bob still did a few spots – usually special interviews for Radio Brassica. Otis was to catch a few of them in the not too distant future.

Sly Stone had been signed to headline, but he pulled out at the last minute, evidently on account of a family affair. He was replaced by The Beach Boys who, in their own way, were almost another family affair. Some locals are on record as seeing them enjoying beers in the Nag's Head pub in Bardney. They must have got in early because the pub totally ran out of beer that weekend. It could, of course, have been Sheffield lad Joe Cocker who drank it all. By all accounts, he was so much the worse for wear that he had to be supported by roadies between songs. It could have been other substances that accounted for his lack of balance of course, but then he never was the most coordinated of performers at the best of times. The good thing for Joe was that he didn't have that far to go home back to Sheffield to sleep it off. That was not the same for some of the other performers. How The Beach Boys must have missed that Californian sun! Billy Joel, Buddy Miles, and Don McLean were also a long way from home.

Rod Stewart, resplendent in a gold jacket, sang with the

Faces, but he spent much of the time complaining about the cold weather. Rory Gallagher, the Groundhogs, Humble Pie, and Slade all went down a storm, though.

As Otis looked closer at the poster he noticed, in the smallest type, the name Genesis. Pretty soon they would be filling stadia all around the world. He thought, *I suppose you've got to start somewhere, and a wet weekend in Lincolnshire is as good a place as any...*

There were a number of late additions to the bill including Wishbone Ash and Roxy Music. Otis marvelled at some of the names of bands from that period: Atomic Rooster, and Wishbone Ash. How do you get to name bands like that? What did they mean? The only thing he could come up with was some kind of occult voodoo ceremony.

As for Roxy Music, it wasn't really the name but rather the exotic nature of the personnel: the suave Geordie, Bryan Ferry and, well, Brian Eno. What could you say? On the inner sleeve of the first Roxy album, Eno, so exotic with his costume and feathers, looked like he'd been brought up by a family of puffins on the Farne Islands. Roxy Music, despite their decadent cabaret look, performed at about eleven o'clock in the morning, to add to the whole surreal nature of the event.

Otis had heard a few interviews with local people because every ten years the local TV channels tended to send a pretty young reporter to stand in a totally empty field in Bardney and say to their teatime audience:

'Ten/twenty/thirty/forty/fifty years ago, in this very field, there was a huge rock festival.'

Then she would list the stellar cast of performers, saying that some, like Sir Rod Stewart, bless him, were still performing today, then cut to the shot of Rod with his lovely wife. The locals would be interviewed and tell of how it had been such an exciting weekend, and that the kids at the festival were lovely.

Another act (not listed on the poster) that appeared was Monty Python's Flying Circus. It turned out that this was their first ever stage performance. It was sadly not recorded how well the dead parrot sketch was received at Bardney in the rain that weekend. *Wow*, thought Otis, *another first that Lincolnshire can chalk up!*

As Otis studied the film of the festival, he thought how Roxy Music were a million miles away from the drab, damp greatcoats worn by most festival-goers. *If only the sun had been shining, we'd have been treated to tie-dyed t-shirts, multi-coloured loon pants and possibly, if Woodstock was anything to go by, nudity and free love.* That would have given the local constabulary something to get exercised about ...

Otis was feeling tired. Staring for too long at his computer screen always had this effect upon him. One last review, he promised himself. Then he'd call it a night.

Barney's Big Adventure – most confusing – till he realised that he'd clicked onto the next site down, which was a review of a kids' film about a dinosaur. *That's the trouble with the damned Internet*, he thought, *it can take you to places you really shouldn't go.* He did notice that the film had been universally panned.

So, rapidly leaving Barney the dinosaur behind, he checked out one last site. It was another local TV report in which a woman said: "All things considered, it hadn't been all that bad, despite the rain". She then went on to say, "After all, we're getting used to all this, what with last year's festival as well".

Otis jerked up from his slumbering posture. Last year? Another festival? Suddenly the research antennae were twitching into overdrive. Further Internet searches revealed an amazing line-up in the same place: Tupholme Manor Park, Bardney, on July twenty-fourth 1971.

The event was billed as the Lincoln Folk Festival. Unlike the 1972 festival where UK acts dominated the bill, this festival was much more evenly balanced, with six UK and seven US acts. This was a high-quality bill of the best contemporary folk artists. Representing the UK were Ralph McTell, Steeleye Span, Pentangle, the Incredible String Band, Sandy Denny (with Richard Thompson), and Dave Swarbrick and Martin Carthy. In the US corner an equally illustrious roster of artists: Tim Hardin, who opened his set with the much covered *Reason to Believe*, Dion, Buffy Sainte Marie, Sonny Terry and Brownie McGhee, Tom Paxton, The Byrds, and James Taylor.

On posters for the event, it read that The Byrds would perform an acoustic set. They hadn't. First song of their all-electric set was *So You Want to be a Rock 'n' Roll Star*.

That's so rock 'n' roll, thought Otis.

As he switched his computer off, he couldn't help thinking how extraordinary Lincolnshire was. Otis was speechless – how had all this gone under the radar? What next? Would he soon find out that Bob Dylan had recovered after his motorcycle accident living in a big pink house in Woodhall Spa? Otis planned to send a couple of researchers out to Bardney to record some interviews with locals ASAP.

CHAPTER 10

Radio Free Brassica

Otis had still not got around to visiting Grimsby, even though it was high on his to-do list. The request to appear on Radio Brassica had come through and, after consulting his Head of School, he was cleared to attend.

He had been assured it was nothing to worry about; just a chat about his impressions of Lincolnshire, and Brassica in particular. On the drive to the radio's studio Otis turned to the station. He caught the end of a trailer advertising the next edition of *Kitchen Kicking*, Radio Brassica's weekly food programme in which food critic, Jay Ranus "batters and deep-fries the TV chefs you love to hate". Jay was also giving away signed, stained shirts from some of his greatest restaurant meals. Next up, Otis was pleased to catch the latest Booming Bob Harris interview. It was another of his Brassica Music Specials, this time with Chris Rea, who was not someone Otis knew much about, so he turned up the volume.

Bob: 'Hi, Chris, good to have you on the show. I know

you've been to Brassica many times.'

Chris: 'Yeah, many times. I've played live many times at the Grimsby Fish Bowl, Scunthorpe Baths, Baytree Garden Centre, and the Boston Starlight Rooms.'

Bob: 'Wow, all the iconic venues! Tell us a bit about your time here.'

Chris: 'Well, December twenty-fourth, two years ago: after the Scunthorpe gig, I was driving home for Christmas. As I left the M180, I joined the A15 towards the Humber Bridge. It was then that I realised *this is the road to Hull*. I pulled over into a layby and wrote that down. It had a certain ring to it. Best Christmas present I've ever had!'

Bob: 'Wow. So it was this side of the Humber, the Lincolnshire side, that inspired your greatest hit song?'

Chris: 'Certainly was. And I'm very grateful to the lad in the Co-op petrol station who gave me directions, because I was all set to go back up the A1.'

Bob: 'Well thanks, Chris. Fascinating as ever talking to you.'

No sooner had Bob's farewell melted into the ether, than Daphne immediately saw another priceless opening to help fill the wide-open spaces of Radio Brassica's schedules.

'Well, thanks again to Bob, and of course to the fabulous Chris Rea. I'll be playing his classic *Road to Hull* later in the show. Now, listeners, let's see how many other songs we can think of with roads, streets or avenues in the title. So, to nearly paraphrase the great U2, let's find where the songs have street names!'

The switchboard went crazy. A couple of American tunes got the ball rolling: *Route 66* and *Highway 61 Revisited*. Gunter from Grimsby chipped in with *Autobahn* by Kraftwerk, but there was no way Daphne, or Radio Brassica for that matter, would consider playing a song that lasted twenty-two minutes and forty-three seconds. To be honest, Gunter hadn't expected it to be played either.

A few Beatles' favourites came, courtesy of Maureen from Goltho – *The Long and Winding Road*, *Blue Jay Way*, and *Penny Lane*.

Daphne cut her off though when she started to say, 'Why don't we do it in the—'

'Please,' interrupted Daphne, 'this is a family show!'

She moved swiftly on to take Bez from Billinghay's *Stan Lee Road*, Paul Weller's song about the creator of *Spiderman*. Gordon from Gedney mentioned The Beatles' *A B-Road*, but Daphne said that was the album title and not a song. Gordon was distraught, so Daphne let him say hello to "everyone that knows me".

The Doors' *Love Street* won Daphne's approval, as did Van Morrison's *Cypress Avenue*. Ray Charles's *Hit the Road, Jack* got the thumbs up too. The Tom Robinson Band's *2-4-6-8 Motorway* got the thumbs down from Daphne, as she pointed out that there wasn't a single mile of motorway in Brassica, and that was how she liked it.

The songs kept rolling in. Stalk 'n' Heads, *The Road to Nowhere* (or Norwich, as Daphne joked) went down well, as did *I'm a Roadrunner* by Bo Diddley, featuring Paula Radcliffe. Canned Heat's *On the Road Again* was a popular choice, as well as *Dead End Street* by The Kinks. Daphne rejected Bob Dylan's *Desolation Row* saying it was too long and too miserable, but let Corinna from Cleethorpes have *Positively 4th Street*. In her quest to be up-beat at all times, Daphne liked the word "positively", saying it had "good vibrations".

Bernie's cousin from Rasen said he couldn't believe nobody had listed *Goodbye Yellow Brick Road*, so he did, and Daphne played it. She then went straight into *The Road to Hull*.

Otis, who had nearly fallen asleep at the wheel, was woken by the opening bars of *Sweet Home Alabama*, a trailer flagging up his appearance on the *Daphne Heckington Show* later that morning. *Nice touch!* he thought. He was always appreciative when people had done their homework.

As Otis entered the radio reception area, he noticed large poster-sized photos of the station's star presenters. The largest by far was Daphne Heckington "The Queen of the Cabbage Patch". She seemed quite a formidable lady.

Otis was shown to the greenroom and given the obligatory iced cabbage smoothie to "settle the nerves". Otis could see through a glass screen into the studio itself and for the first time he saw Daphne in action.

She was interviewing a guy called Chris Packham, evidently a nationally known environmentalist, who happened to be presenting a *Nature Watch* special on TV from Lincolnshire all this week. It was clear that Daphne was enjoying sparring with Chris. Evidently, he'd been on the show last year and had caused a major controversy in Brassica and beyond. This is what Daphne lived for – a guest who set the switchboard on fire!

Chris had accused the farming industry of rendering the humble cabbage white butterfly almost extinct.

In a debate with farmer Jim Gedney of Gedney Drain, Chris had been told in no uncertain terms: 'If it's cabbage whites or cabbages, then it's got to be cabbages every time. It's our livelihood that tree-hugger is threatening!'

Daphne briefly referred to this, but said she wouldn't be taking calls on that topic today; only things relating to Chris's shows this week.

She was certainly giving him a hard time, reminding him that she was a Brassica girl through and through. Chris's theme that day was about endangered and invasive species. He talked about red and grey squirrels, and our native white-clawed crayfish that was in serious decline as the bigger and more aggressive American Robert Crayfish was taking over.

Chris said he was also hoping to see the famous Lincolnshire red sparrow which is a species that had adapted remarkably well to their new habitats. It was believed they had frequently been spotted over Scampton and now Waddington. These birds flew in amazingly tight formation. It was believed that they did this in order to deter predators that thought they were combatting one large bird, as opposed to several smaller ones. Chris said another thing these remarkable birds did when under attack was to discharge coloured gas from their rear ends in order to confuse their predators. Chris said they were hoping to catch this on film for the first time that week. Chris finished off by saying that there was a pair of green falcon nesting on top of Lincoln Cathedral and they were hoping to film activity at close quarters with a "nest-cam".

Daphne was a little disappointed that there was nothing controversial from Chris this time to set the switchboard off, so she wound up the interview and said goodbye to him.

She played *Freebird* by Lynyrd Skynyrd, a clever choice she thought, linking Chris the naturalist, and Otis the academic from Alabama. (She also had a habit of playing it when not currently in a relationship and about to interview an unattached handsome guy.) She had done some preliminary research of her own on Professor Otis K. Spanner, and she definitely liked what she saw through the control room window.

Otis was quietly ushered into Daphne's studio during the long and, to be honest, rather tedious guitar solo.

Daphne started. 'My next guest has travelled several thousand miles to come and spend a whole year of his life here in beautiful Brassica. So it's a very warm welcome to Professor Otis Spanner!'

Otis said, 'Thank y'all for making me so welcome. I have to say, I'm loving it here. Lincolnshire has exceeded my expectations, many times over. The richness of the musical heritage is truly amazing!' Otis, feeling more confident, now added, 'I do hope, Miss Heckington, ma'am, you don't think I'm one of those horrible invasive species that needs putting down?'

'Oh please, call me Daphne,' she simpered. 'And no, you are most welcome here, as I've already said.'

Otis said, 'Back home in Alabama, we know how to control crawfish and squirrels: the hillbilly crackers – the country folks – they just eats 'em!'

The switchboard immediately lit up with outraged Brassicans (who usually raged against the invading hordes of grey squirrels) but were now apoplectic over the idea that anyone would have the bad taste to actually eat the dammed things.

As Otis racked his brain for his grandma's squirrel fricassee recipe, he noticed a furious Chris Packham banging his fists on the glass control room window.

Daphne muttered something about cultural differences and quickly moved on to Otis's musical research. She asked Otis what he had been most impressed by so far. Otis mentioned that there was far too much significant stuff to single any one thing out at present, but he did say that he really enjoyed his visit to Cultural Mick's in Boston and that he was hoping to return there very soon.

The interview came to a close and Daphne, sensing an opportunity, said it was a long time since she'd been to

Cultural Mick's and maybe she could join him on his next visit.

Otis, who always liked to do primary research on his own terms, made appropriately pleasant but rather vague noises.

When Otis went outside, there was a *save our squirrels* protest in full swing and his car had been plastered with *save our squirrels* and *nobody eats our squirrels* stickers.

'Ah, the joys of local radio,' said Otis as his thoughts now turned to his date with Grimsby.

When back in his office to quickly refresh his memory by reading the Grimsby file, he'd been interrupted by a call from a somewhat angry Head of School. She said the VC was incandescent with rage having heard the interview. Evidently, there had been a plan to invite Chris Packham to be a guest lecturer. The university had been plying him with cases of fatballs and boxes of Trill for years, and Otis, not to put too fine a point on it, had put a spanner in the works.

Otis mumbled a few niceties, saying he'd not meant to cause any offence and that he'd thought the interview had gone rather well. Next up, as they say on the radio, Grimsby. Or so he thought...

CHAPTER 11

Market Rasen (Again)

As Otis got in his car and studied his sat nav, he noticed that in order to get to Grimsby he had to drive through Market Rasen again. This was fortuitous as he needed to finish off a few things, and intended calling in to meet the archivist (invariably the longest serving history teacher) at the De Aston school.

As was customary on these road trips, Otis switched on Radio Brassica. They were celebrating Lincolnshire and Brassica food and music month with a series of special interviews, of course hosted by local favourite Booming Bob Harris.

Otis just caught the beginning of what turned out to be a fascinating talk with Terry Vegetables, the former England football team manager.

Bob: 'My very special guest today is no stranger to Brassica. It's Terry Vegetables, the footballer and ex-England manager. Some of our listeners may know that Terry has a luxury double caravan on the exclusive Gibraltar Point complex. Tel popped into our studios earlier today and I recorded this chat with him:

Bob: 'Hi, how did you end up having a home in Lincolnshire?'

TV: 'My agent said Gibraltar Point was a great deal, so I signed on the dotted line. To be brutally honest, I thought it was nearer Spain. But I've been coming for years now and I've grown to love it. Especially now I've learnt the language – that's a big bonus.'

Bob: 'You're a man of many talents, Tel. With all your football achievements, I think people tend to forget that you are a writer and singer, too.'

TV: 'That's very true, Bob. Not too many football managers have had a chart hit like mine.'

Bob: 'Reached number twenty-three, I believe, in 2010. The great Elvis song *If I Can Dream*.

TV: 'Would have gone higher, if it hadn't had Harry Redknapp and Wrighty croaking in the background ha-ha!'

Bob: 'We know you are a big music and food fan, too. If we are to believe the tabloids, you eat two or sometimes three meals a day. What are you favourite songs associated with this region?'

TV: 'I was at Chelsea in the Swinging Sixties and I used to dance down the King's Road to some cracking tunes. I remember twisting with Chopper Harris. He's no relation is he, Bob?'

Bob: 'I believe he's my father's second cousin once removed.'

TV: 'Once removed? He was frequently being "removed" – sent off, I mean! Some of those tackles... He nearly cut Billy Bremner in half. Happy days, eh?'

Bob: 'Indeed. Now, back to the music, Tel. Give us some of your favourite tunes.'

TV: As I was saying, *Twist and Sprout* by The Beatles. *A Whiter Shade of Kale*, great song. *Green Onions* – top, top tune. More recently, I really like Eurythmics' *Swede Dreams*, but I always think ABBA should have done that one. *Monster Mash* always goes down well at our Halloween parties. But I think my all-time favourite was The Beatles' song from the early days: *Long Tall Salad*.

Bob: 'That brings us on to healthy eating. As a sportsman, I'm sure you know a thing or two about that. In our recent Salad Special, Roger Poultry of The Who told us he was definitely a chicken Caesar man. Paul McCartney, after meeting Linda, became a big lettuce fan, as witnessed by his great song *Lettuce B*. Even chose the same name for the last album!

TV: 'Funny you should say that because I was chatting to Elton John about salads when he was still chairman of Watford, at the 1984 cup final when they lost two – nil to Everton. Elton told me that without a shadow of a doubt, when it came to salads he was definitely a rocket man.

Bob: 'Well, great talking to you, Tel, and give my regards to the beautiful Gibraltar Point.'

Fascinating stuff, thought Otis. *Plenty of food for thought there.*

There were a few more people about in Market Rasen this time, some of them on horseback. *Must be a race day*, Otis thought. The school was close by the racetrack. Otis parked and went inside.

The school archivist at De Aston was very helpful in supplying Otis with dates and other tit-bits of information about Rod Temperton's schooldays. Bernie, it transpired, had not gone to De Aston; unlike his brother Tony and Rod, he'd been a pupil at Market Rasen Secondary Modern School. Bernie had left as soon as he could, aged fifteen. Rod, on the other hand, shone as a musical star at De Aston. He used to play the drums, and he always used to enter the school music competitions, often winning of course as he was a great all-round musician.

Just as Otis was packing up his things, Miss Waltham said there was another boy he might want to look up who went on to do well for himself. His time overlapped with Rod's time at school.

'He may have some reminisces that you might be able to use.' She pointed to a school photograph and Otis saw a bespectacled youth. Underneath it read: *Grahame Lloyd*.

'Why is there an extra vowel in his first name?' asked Otis.

'Originally Welsh, I believe,' hazarded Miss Waltham. 'Lloyd is definitely a Welsh name.'

She told Otis that Mr Lloyd had become a journalist, radio producer and presenter, sports commentator, and author of several books. She said that he also ran a media company that covered publishing, radio, and TV and film production.

Jeez, thought Otis, *sound like a proper Maxwell, or Murdoch. Definitely someone I need to talk to.*

Latterly, she said he had taken up a career as a poet and singer-songwriter, doing several one-man UK tours. *Wow*, thought Otis. *Amazing!*

'Wow. How come I've never heard of him?' said Otis.

'Well, he's a bit like Rod, really. He keeps a very low profile. You could say another "invisible man". Also, he does go on rather about cricket, something which hasn't really taken root in America.'

The only crickets Otis knew about were the insects, and the ones that had come from Lubbock in Texas and had stood behind Buddy Holly.

'I think he's on the mailing list for the school magazine. I can look up his contact details for you if you like? I'm sure he wouldn't mind.'

Otis was pleased to accept. When she returned, he noticed that the address was in Cardiff, the Welsh capital.

Singer-songwriter, Otis mused. *What is it about this place? And all three with links to a small Lincolnshire town, quite frankly in the middle of nowhere! Must be something in the water...*

Not that he said that to the helpful Miss Waltham.

'Can I get to hear some of his songs?'

Miss Waltham said that Lloyd was a very private person when not performing, and she didn't think he'd actually recorded them for wider consumption. She also added that she was sure he would have his own private recordings if Otis wanted to contact him.

She said he was clearly a serious performer as before every show, he always made a three hundred and eighty-two-mile round trip to Lincoln just to have his guitar restrung and tuned by an "expert".

Otis thanked Miss Waltham, and gave her one of his new cards in case she remembered anything else she thought he ought to know.

Once in the car he phoned the office and asked Mary to contact the local radio station to see if they had any more information on Grahame Lloyd.

He got a call back about ten minutes later saying that he was known to them; his last appearance evidently about some cricket ball he seemed to have lost. *Cricket again*, thought Otis. *I must get someone to explain what that's all about.*

It appears that someone at the radio station knew someone who'd played golf regularly with Mr Lloyd. There was some speculation that he'd gone back to Wales after being invited to be resident professional at Celtic Manor. Someone else volunteered the information that he also returned to Lincoln on a regular basis to have his hair cut.

Otis thought, *I'm clearly dealing with a guy who looks after his appearance if he's also willing to make a three hundred and eighty-two-mile round-trip to get a short-back-and-sides. Extraordinary. Must be one helluva hairstyle to justify a trip like that.*

Otis later discovered from some sources in a hostelry, not a million miles from the castle wall, that the attraction to the place was more prosaic. One morning, Mr L had arrived rather earlier than usual for his appointment, on account of having to go to Stoke to commentate on a pointless Aunt Bessie Smith's Instant Custard cup-tie later in the day (pointless because it was a dead rubber, allegedly like the custard when it went cold). Much to his surprise and horror, he discovered Luigi, his Italian barber, in delicto flagrante with Glenis from the flower shop next door. In exchange for his vow of *omertà*, he was promised free haircuts for life, and flowers, at a very generous thirty-five per cent discount should he ever need either.

Before leaving, Miss Waltham said she'd managed to find a number for Mr Lloyd, and Otis called him. It was a FaceTime call, and Otis had caught him out and about in Cardiff. Otis noticed the trim haircut, and a large imposing building that he made out to be the local university judging by the logo atop the building: *It's Brains we Want.*

Mr L was very helpful in talking about his time at school and he filled in a few details about Rod Temperton's musical activities. Grahame said that his own modest performing career was now at an end and that if Otis wanted to talk further or buy any of his books, he had a hair appointment in eight weeks and he would be over for a trim in Lincoln then.

'Such a nice guy,' said Otis, as he reflected on what had been another busy day.

Miss Waltham had been most helpful. *Indeed a real star*, thought Otis, and he would definitely be thanking her in the introduction when he finally got round to publishing the book of his Brassica adventures.

By now, the race day traffic had seriously built up and Miss Waltham advised giving Grimsby a miss as Otis would not have enough time to take in all the sights and musical heritage that lay there. She suggested at least a whole day was needed, and why didn't he go on the train instead? Otis said he'd consider the idea, but thought that he'd really miss the informative Radio Brassica music specials. Miss Waltham suggested headphones and why not let the train take the strain. Definitely tomorrow, without fail, Grimsby by rail.

CHAPTER 12

The Day Train to Cleethorpes and Grimsby

As the Cleethorpes train pulled in to Lincoln station, the guard shouted, 'All aboard!'

Otis was immediately reminded of what he thought was probably the best train song ever – *Night Train* by James Brown and the Famous Flames. It started with Brown shouting, "All aboard!" and he then proceeded to list all stations north from Miami, Florida to Boston, Massachusetts. That was it, nothing else; the song merely a roll call of stations as the train sped north through the night. It should have been tedious beyond belief, but it wasn't. It was one of James's finest grooves, with a killer saxophone solo to boot.

This was the first time Otis had been on a train since his ill-fated trip to London. Again, it was one of the rattling tin-type contraptions, but the journey was not unpleasant. He could look out on the Witham Valley before the train swung inland towards Market Rasen.

The train briefly stopped there, and Otis smiled as he

remembered his detective work on the *Tumbleweed Connection* album cover. He'd decided to stay on the train to the end of the line at Cleethorpes, as he'd discovered that Rod Temperton was actually born and raised there.

Cleethorpes was a bit of a surprise to Otis. As soon as he got off the train, he noticed that there was a pub actually on the railway platform. *That's quite a welcome*, he thought, *but not now. Maybe later in the day perhaps, after the important work of capturing the area's undoubted contribution to popular culture.*

Otis found that for such a hugely successful person, Rod Temperton had kept a remarkably low profile. Not for nothing was one of his nicknames "the invisible man". One thing he hadn't hidden though was his extraordinary talent. Evidence of his songs were everywhere. Jukeboxes around the globe had throbbed to his funky compositions and arrangements. *Thriller* might well have a claim to be the most popular tune in the world, having sold over sixty-five million copies, but what's more, Rod had written three of the nine songs on the album. Not bad going for a lad from Cleethorpes whose first job upon leaving De Aston in Market Rasen was to work in the Ross frozen fish factory in neighbouring Grimsby.

A thought came to Otis: *Ross?* He wondered whether Diana Ross had any Grimsby connections. He had quickly come to learn that Lincolnshire was capable of the greatest surprises when it came to popular music.

It had come to Otis's attention that Bernie T had written a

song for Elton's *Caribou* album called *Grimsby*, which is really a love song for the place. Clearly, many of Bernie's formative experiences took place here, judging by the wistful, nostalgic lyrics.

Otis had been thinking about this as the train neared the place itself. He noted that *Grimsby* joins a very select list of songs with just a geographical place name as a title. Most of the ones he could remember were back home in the US: Randy Newman's *Birmingham*, Scott Mackenzie's *San Francisco*, Eric Burdon's *Monterey*, and Old Blue Eyes's *Chicago* and *New York, New York*. He also remembered another from north Alabama, near the Shoals, a Drive-by Trucker's number called *Zip City*. (Yes, believe it or not, there really is a place called Zip City!) But *Grimsby* was the only UK song that fitted the bill. Mike Oldfield's *Portsmouth* is an instrumental, so technically doesn't count as a song. So, that's another first for Lincolnshire!

Bernie mentioned a pub, The Skinners' Arms, in the song. Otis wondered if it was still there. He would ask around.

He had made an appointment to meet Tom Crabbe, a journalist from the *Grimsby Telegraph*, in a small café overlooking the fish docks. It reminded him a little of Monterey in California, but without the sea lions and the sunshine. Tom was a real ambassador for Grimsby and he gave Otis a comprehensive tour of the area. First stop was the Cleethorpes pier, home of some legendary soul all-nighters in the '70s and '80s. Alas, there was no Skinners' Arms – Bernie must have made it up!

An example of the poetic licence trade, thought Otis.

He then showed Otis the pub where the Grimsby folk club met, and told him about some of the famous acts who had played there. Martin Carthy and the Watersons had made the long trip from Hull in the days before the bridge. Not being able to see a bridge, Otis let that pass. Tom then said that Paul Simon had played the club in 1965. Not only that, he had played there twice, and on one occasion had turned up on the wrong night and played for free! Evidently, he went down quite well, though some locals thought him a bit of a "flash Harry" on account of his shoes.

'Shoes?' said Otis.

'Yeah,' said Tom. 'Looked like he'd got diamonds on the soles of his shoes.'

'Wow. I'll bet he must have had a very expensive carbon footprint,' said Otis, feeling rather proud of his quick retort.

'It's more likely that it was one of those pubs that always had glass on the floor,' added Tom. 'At one time, when the trawler fleets were home, there were plenty of pubs in Grimsby with sticky, sparkly carpets!'

Tom then said he couldn't stay long as he had to go to the Grimsby Fish Bowl because the town was expecting a special announcement about the government's "levelling up" agenda.

Tom explained that Grimsby was the home of UK grime music. It had been pioneered by Rod Temperton's cousin Tinie Temper and his mate Dave from Tetney. Tom said it wasn't really his kind of music, but it was massively popular with the kids. Grime acts always sold out at the Fish Bowl.

The council had started a campaign to get people to love Grimsby by using high pressure hoses to clean slogans into the grime on the street and pavements. Looking round, Otis wondered why they didn't just clean the streets, period.

Tom also said, as they arrived at the Fish Bowl, that tribute bands went down very well in Grimsby. Codplay were obviously popular, as was that tribute band from Cornwall, Cornish Pastiche.

Otis had been thinking about the amazing fact that Paul Simon had played Grimsby twice in the '60s. He seemed to remember a *Rolling Stone* interview that Art Garfunkel had given, saying that he always regretted not playing the town.

He'd suggested it several times, but Paul had said, "No, been there, done that – twice".

Art had hinted that this was why they ended up going their separate ways. Alas, for them there was no Humber Bridge over troubled waters.

While they were waiting for the press conference, Tom regaled Otis with a few more music anecdotes. Did Otis know, for example, that U2's Larry Mullet was rumoured to have been born, or at least landed, in Grimsby? He also told of the time where there was a plan to stop producing frozen cod in parsley sauce and there were riots around the fish docks. Those trouble-makers from Brigg, The Beastly Boys, even wrote a song for the march: *Fight for Your Right to Parsley*. The company backed down, and now it's one of their bestsellers.

There was some movement on the stage and Otis notice that the junior minister he had met on the train on the way to London, had obviously been given his moment to shine in public. He started:

'As you know, there was much disappointment when the new Tate gallery proposals hit insurmountable difficulties, and had to be relocated elsewhere.'

(The minister, having called in the plans for further consultation decided, after due consideration, that the whole scheme was far too "arty-farty" for those cabbage-heads in Brassica, and he quietly scheduled it to open in his own Surrey constituency. He felt that it, and he, would benefit from this judicious decision. In return, he had approved planning permission for the attached restaurant and retail complex that, coincidentally, was to be built on a parcel of land adjacent to the busy A17 belonging to a Mrs Gladys Dogdyke, head of a well-known and respected local cabbage farming dynasty, who apparently, quite by chance, happened to be the chair of the local party.)

The minister was now getting into his stride, mentioning a subject close to his heart: "Levelling Up for Grimsby". He was pleased to announce that Grimsby, or Great Grimsby to give it its proper and much deserved name, had been granted the *Lion King*'s share of the Elton John platform shoe horde, which had been recently discovered and excavated from a series of Thames-side lock-up garages near Windsor. The minister said that he really believed that this would help raise the aspirations of struggling young people in Grimsby, and help them stand tall, and brighten up their dull little lives. There was a round of applause, and 'hear, hear' from the platform party.

The minister went on:

'I know you've had it hard here for some time, what with all the unemployment after the Icelanders came and stole all the fish from the freezer warehouses and started the Cod War.'

The minister was on a roll and he just kept talking.

'People in Grimsby have had to eat haddock for far too long, and in order to end the Cod War this government was going to pass a cod law, making haddock more expensive, so that market forces would work in favour of stabilising the price of cod to make it more affordable for hard-working, ordinary eaters of fish and fish fingers. Also, there would be a batter tax, but only on sausages, thus encouraging people to go back to cod.'

Everybody cheered and the local MP said this was what the town needed, and it was just the boost Grimsby had been asking for.

'But,' she added, 'would the minister consider forcing the town's kebab shops to start selling cod, too?'

The minister thanked her, saying that this was just the kind of constructive comment that would truly make Grimsby great again.

Again, great applause.

After the meeting, Tom said he would walk Otis to the train

station. Otis couldn't help but admire the splendid architecture of the Grimsby Fish Bowl, a truly iconic structure. Otis thought its only rival was the Bird's Nest Soup Bowl in Beijing, or possibly the Cereal Bowl in Winnipeg, Canada.

The Fish Bowl, in its relatively short life, had played host to some major and memorable acts. LA-based band, Eels, loved it here, as did Codplay. Marillion always played well here, but then they did have Fish as their lead singer. And who wasn't still talking about last month's great concert, where Carole King-Prawn played the whole of *Tap-History*, her concept album on the development of domestic water delivery systems? The whole place was awash with praise.

But the Fish Bowl is really the spiritual home of the biggest and "baddest" UK grime festival, which is held each January, traditionally the grimmest of winter months. The show went on all day long, with non-stop grimacing from all concerned. To give a flavour of the quality on show, the last gig had started with Giggs, then the Little Nasty, Medium Nasty and Big Narstie. Next up, Yo Mutha, and local boys Yo Sushi and Tinie Tempura. More nasty stuff with Nasty Jack, Big Gob and Loudmouth, then back to a bit of normality with Dan, Danny B and Dave. The Fish Bowl was the grimiest place, and all the big fish wanted to swim in that tank.

Otis thanked Tom for guiding him around town. He caught the train back to Lincoln from Grimsby station, but alas, no pub on the platform there.

He put in his earphones and tuned into *The Daphne*

Heckington Show. Daphne was on cloud nine as she had just completed her annual stint presenting *The Daphne Heckington Show live* from the famous Heckington Show. Clearly, some people were born to do local radio! She was inviting listeners to phone in to help her make up her food-football all-stars eleven. Evidently, this had been inspired by Terry Vegetable's recent appearance on Brassica FM.

It had already been established that Tel was to be director of football, and the manager was Barry Fry-Up (he'd been preferred to Kenny Jacket-Potato). Peter Stilton was everyone's choice for keeper.

Karen from Coningsby suggested Ledley Burger-King at the heart of the defence, but others said he was always injured, so perhaps he should be on the bench. Carlton Palmer-Ham made the cut, as did Brain Éclair and Tony Panna-Cottee. Trevor Cherry and Pat Rice were also in the frame. Brian Flann, the Welsh midget-gem, got a mention too.

Daphne said, 'Keep 'em coming and we'll invite Tel and Barry Fry-Up into the studio next week to pick their strongest team.'

None of this made much sense to Otis, but he had to admire Daphne's stamina at keeping up such a frenetic pace. By goodness, she was good at her job. He admired that.

CHAPTER 13

Louth, the Laurel Canyon of Lincs

Otis's researchers had been getting increasingly excited by what they were discovering about Louth; a small market town about twenty-five miles from Lincoln. Louth was in the Lincolnshire Wolds, an area of gentle green hills and valleys, not at all like the flat, wet plains of Brassica to the south. Otis also had discovered that there was a good vinyl record shop there called Off the Beaten Tracks. Otis really liked the name, and even considered it as an appropriate title for the book he was hoping to publish after that year of intensive research. So far he'd been astounded by the things he'd uncovered, and couldn't wait to reveal to the wider world just how important Lincolnshire's contribution to music and popular culture had been. "Under the radar" and "off the beaten track" had just about summed it up. *But how that perception will change*, he thought, *when my work is finally done here.*

As usual, Otis tuned in to Brassica FM, his now faithful companion on his sometimes lonely research trips. It was

Bombastic Bob "Bomber" Harris Jr's star interview – the one the station had been advertising for weeks as the highlight of the Brassica Food and Music Festival.

Bob: 'I'm so delighted to say that today's guest, no stranger to Brassica, is real rock royalty. Welcome Mr Keith Richards! Keith, what first brought you to Brussels Shoals?'

Keith: 'Well, when we were playing on Eel Pie Island, Mick heard about this great restaurant doing interesting things with sprouts, somewhere up north near Boston. Mick was all set to fly to the States to check it out, when my assistant, Jack Daniels, said it wasn't that Boston, it was the one in Fen land. Mick was about to fly to Helsinki, when we got a message to divert the plane to Brassica. When he finally splashed down in the wetlands, he said the food was great, so the whole band came up here.'

Bob: 'I gather you hired your own personal chef, after spending some time here?'

Keith: 'Yeah, when we tour the States, we all have our own personal chefs – we like to have a taste of home while on these long tours. Bill, the Lincolnshire poacher, does all my eggs these days. When you get to our age you know what you like and what agrees with you.'

Bob: 'So, when did you first come up here?'

Keith: 'About a hundred and twenty years ago, I think.'

Bob: 'And you keep coming back.'

Keith: 'Well, the sprouts are so good, man. Best in the world!'

Bob: 'And you started recording here. How did that come about?'

Keith: 'We found a little recording shack in Brussels Shoals and I had this idea for a song about all those crazy parties we'd been going to in London – *Wild Houses* it was called.'

Bob: 'How did that work out?'

Keith: 'When we first came here, it was so long ago that the farmers worked the land with horse-drawn ploughs – real big heavy horses. So, I changed the lyrics to *Wide Horses*, and we cut the track.'

Bob: 'Wow! So that song was literally inspired by your Brassica experience?'

Keith: 'Sure was!'

Bob: 'That song has a definite country feel to it. Tell us how that came about.'

Keith: 'Well, this cat, Gram Parsnips, a local boy, showed me how to play in the local style. After a couple of hours doing sprouts, everything takes on a kind of wind – swept laidback country vibe, I still love it. Couldn't drag me away!'

Bob: 'I was going to thank Keith and give him a high five, but as you may have heard in the media recently, Keith has donated his hands to the Natural History Museum in London, and is currently awaiting delivery of a new pair before the band's centenary American tour next year. Good luck with all that and thumbs up... Oops! Sorry, Keith! Thanks for sharing your memories of a very special part of the world.

'Now on next week's show we have an exclusive special

performance from U2's The Hedge, and Kate Bush, live from the Lawn in Lincoln. Can't wait! Don't miss it!'

Otis was certainly impressed with the top quality performers who came to this part of the UK.

The road was definitely hilly and, in the distance, he could see the tall spire of St James's church in Louth. It was market day in Louth, and Otis felt the buzz of a busy bustling town. He noted some small local shops and a few of the usual charity shops. *This looks like a place with real possibilities*, thought Otis.

He had already heard that a number of musicians had settled in the area and that there were quite a few recording studios in the little valleys and villages round about. Lincoln's Laurel Canyon, he'd heard it called. Paul Weller – the hardest Woking man in rock – had been sighted on several occasions.

There was Chapel Studios in South Thoresby, evidently a great residential complex for those who wanted to get away from it all and get high on the lovely Lincolnshire countryside. Their clients included Arctic Monkeys, The Streets, Paul Weller, Simple Minds, and Barbara Dickson the Scottish singer who used to live nearby before returning to Edinburgh.

In Louth itself, he learned about the Sweet Factory Studios which was run by the former Magazine and Visage member, Dave Formula, and his two kids, Magic and Secret. It was evidently a very tidy place with a very clean sound, as apparently Dave was very big on the correct use of soap. Dave still played in two local bands: The Legendary Night Hawks, and Dave Formula and the Finks. *Never heard of them*, thought Otis. A bit more research turned up that Dave also went by the name Dave Tomlinson. Otis didn't know whether his kids had other names as well. Yet another studio, The Pump House, was situated even a little bit further off the beaten track.

The first place to visit, so that Otis could get his bearings, was Off the Beaten Tracks itself. It was everything Otis had hoped it would be – a great little record shop with an owner who was passionate about music. Otis thought he was probably the most enthusiastic and polite record store owner he'd ever encountered, anywhere. He was genuinely thanked for coming in to the shop, thanked for taking an interest, and thanked for actually making a purchase. With all that thanking going on, Otis felt it would be rude to leave without putting a little cash across the counter. But in truth it wasn't difficult, as the stock was great, the prices good, and the service second to none. The shop was owned by Mark Merrifield and his wife Lee Conybeare. Otis thought that with a name like that, she could have leaped straight out of a Father John Misty song.

If only all record stores had such a welcoming approach, thought Otis, *the world would be a better place.*

Otis had been so busy recently writing up his findings that he had fallen a little behind with his forward planning. His team had been brilliant at initial background research, producing outlines and possible lines of enquiry for him to follow, but he needed to draw breath and finish reading the briefing papers they'd provided on Louth.

He needed a coffee, and his eye settled on an arty-looking place called Crackpots. *Just the place*, he thought, *to order my favourite Skinny Africano and quietly finish the Louth briefing*. The place seemed quite busy with people who seemed to have wandered in off the street, happy to get their hands dirty, rummaging about in buckets of what appeared to be mud.

Everyone seemed OK, and Otis noticed an elegant woman sitting at a table smiling away and an old guy in a wheelchair muttering about larders, jammy jars and mustard. As he waited to order his Skinny Africano, he suddenly had a thought. *Crackpots – this isn't some kind of care-in-the community drop-in centre, is it?* The clientele all seemed happy enough: dirty-handed types, engaged with coil pots, slab pots, and even the odd bust. One guy, sitting near the window wearing two badges, both proclaiming Gordon is a moron, looked particularly strange. One badge was bad enough, but two certainly seemed somewhat over the top to Otis. What was all that about? Could you just walk in, or did you have to be referred here? As he was thinking of slip-sliding away, a kind-looking woman asked how she could help.

'Bit of a crisis,' she said. 'Robert Whynot's head exploded in the kiln yesterday and we're still finding bits of him all over the place.'

'Robert Whynot?' said Otis, clearly confused. '*The* Robert Whynot, who was in Daft Machine in the '60s? The drummer, the singer – the guy who worked with the legendary Ivor Cutler?'

'Well, yes, that's him. In fact, he was in here earlier.' She looked beyond Otis before saying, 'Oh, he must have gone.'

Otis noticed that the old guy muttering about larders and jammy jars, and the woman next to him, had both obviously just left.

The café owner, Elaine, explained that she was a sculptor and potter, and that she occasionally took commissions. She would sculpt a head in clay and then glaze and fire it in the kiln out in the back. She'd recently done a bust of Robert but in the firing process something had gone catastrophically wrong. Crackpots all over the shop!

'So,' said Otis, 'I've just missed meeting one of the true originals of British alternative rock culture?'

'Oh, don't worry, dear,' said Elaine. 'He and Alfie are always around. He often pops in for a drink and a chat. They only live down the street.'

'Was that the woman with him earlier?'

'Yes, she's lovely. She did all the artwork for Robert's solo albums; really cool stuff. A great team they are,' said Elaine.

She then told Otis about the time that Bjork, the queen of Iceland, visited Louth to see Robert, and how some old dears, hearing about it on the local radio, thought she'd come to open a frozen food supermarket. Other musical friends had visited too, including Paul Weller on several occasions. He didn't open a supermarket, either.

Robert, despite the number of recording studios in Louth, recorded most of his 2007 album *Comicopera* at his home studio in the centre of town, only a matter of yards from where Otis was now sitting with his third Skinny Africano.

When he set off that morning, he'd not expected to uncover all that about such a unique performer. Otis thought again about how Lincolnshire had this enormous capacity to spring surprises. It really did remind him of back home in northern Alabama. How come so many great and diverse performers had ended up in Muscle Shoals on the banks of the Tennessee River, recording timeless music in the middle of apparently nowhere?

After delving further into his briefing notes, he learned that Louth had another pop music connection, as Corinne Drewery, the lead signer with the sophisti-pop '80s band Swing Out Sister had gone to school in Louth, before going to Lincoln College and then on to study fashion in London. Another part of Corinne's musical education had taken place on the famous Cleethorpes pier, where she had regularly attended its famous northern soul nights.

Otis saw the man with the badges get up and shuffle out into the street. Otis moved towards the counter and his curiosity got the better of him.

He couldn't stop himself asking Elaine, 'That fellow who's just left – what's with the badges' slogan Gordon is a moron? Is there some kind of local vendetta going on?'

'Oh, that's Graham, though sometimes he likes to be called

John. Depends which side of the bed he gets out of, I think. Bit of a comedian; bit of an acquired taste, if you ask me. I think he lives out near the garden centre somewhere. He's what they call one of those one-hit wonders. In the '70s he had a traumatic experience and wrote a song about it: *Jilted John*. It got to number four in the UK chart in 1978. *Gordon is a moron* – that's the chorus of the song. You can check it out on YouTube.'

Otis thought she had to be pulling his leg. Not quite knowing what to think, he got ready to pay.

Elaine, who'd just come off the phone, said to anyone who was listening, 'The boss is not well.'

Otis, who'd gained the impression that Elaine was the boss around here, could only mutter, 'Oh dear, sorry to hear that,' as he handed over his cash. So, it was time to make tracks back to Lincoln and the office.

Back in the car, Daphne Heckington was still pouring out of the radio with her usual upbeat enthusiasm. Following on from the Keith Richards exclusive interview, she was urging her devoted listeners to call in and giver her as many pop stars whose names were made up of two forenames, like for example George Michael or Paul Simon.

The Brassica musical cognoscenti showered the airwaves with names: Chris Martin, Les Paul, Craig David, Jack Bruce, Celine Dion, Dean Martin, Deborah Harry, Nina Simone, and the favourite, by far, Vera Lynn. Otis threw Duane Eddy into the mix, thinking, *at least it helps pass the time when out on the road*. With that, he arrived back in Lincoln.

CHAPTER 14

Back to the Cabbage Studio, Washing and Bob's

It was time for Otis to return to the top-secret Cabbage Studios complex to learn more about the show that Gina Broccoli said was going to be the next big thing.

He met up with Reg Carvery again and they travelled into deepest Brassica, passing through Gedney this and Gedney that. At one point they passed through Gedney Hill, which quite frankly to Otis didn't seem very much like a hill at all, given that its maximum elevation came in at around the five metre mark, or as Otis like to think, just a tad over sixteen feet.

Reg told Otis about the elite Gedney Hill mountain rescue team, a kind of special force for Brassica, on-call 24/7, but never really been called out since the year 1216 when King John was reputed to have lost his baggage train in The Wash. The mountain rescue team were based at the nearby Gedney Hill Golf Club, where they enjoyed honorary membership, reduced green fees and discounted golf balls.

Reg said they had legendary skills and were masters of

disguise. They often appeared at the Great Brassica Show, but few had actually seen them; so good were they at disguise. A particular skill was their ability to don tight-fitting rubber suits and to move silently, like eels, across the Fens.

As with all special services, it was the element of surprise that rendered them so effective, that and their ability to blend totally into their environment. The famous Stealth-Eels were obviously the inspiration for the US Navy Seals, whose somewhat inscrutable motto was: The only easy day was yesterday. Otis preferred Tomorrow never knows, the Gedney Hill team's motto. *Actually*, he thought, *on reflection, neither make any sense at all...* But who was he to question military intelligence, or any other oxymoron for that matter?

Still, Otis was suitably impressed and asked if it would be possible to meet up with these special people. Reg said he'd heard they were otherwise engaged at a golf tournament at that moment and were therefore out of contact.

As they had an hour or two to kill before meeting Ms Broccoli, Reg suggested they make the short journey to visit the legendary' Bob's Records in Whittlesey. Otis was overjoyed – he'd been meaning to go for some time. This was one of the key corners of the Vinyl Triangle.

Whittlesey had a McCain's chip factory, a brickworks with huge chimneys, and Bob's Records, which was next-door-but-one from a very good butcher who sold extremely imaginative sausage rolls and, more surprisingly, excellent Eccles cakes. (Surprisingly, because it's a very long way from Eccles.)

Bob was a bit of an institution in those parts. If it had been recorded on vinyl, he'd know about it and, what's more, if he hadn't got it, he'd know where to get it from. Bob also claimed that, "If it has a hole in the middle, then I sells it", which was why he always stocked Polo mints and a fine selection of bagels and doughnuts (the ring kind, of course, not the tennis ball-sized ones covered in sugar and injected with jam).

Bob's business card was adorned with his personal logo which featured strongly his trademark spectacles. Probably Buddy Holly, Roy Orbison, and Eric Morecombe were the only three celebrity specky-four-eyes who were as recognisable as Bob.

Bob's Records called itself an independent record shop, and must have been one of the best organised shops anywhere. Otis was impressed with the stock, its range and quality. Even Bob's assistant, who sometimes stood in when the great man was busy transporting fish tanks full of fish to their new home near Long Sutton, made Otis feel at home by telling him of record buying trips to Memphis and the South.

Just spending half an hour in the shop was a real education. Bob had a lifetime of stories with which he regaled regulars and newcomers alike. Everybody was made to feel welcome, and if you had a music related question and it was on vinyl, then Bob was your man. Bob's shop was on Broad Street in Whittlesey, and it was thought, by many in the know, that Paul McCartney's *Give My Regards to Broad Street* referred to Bob's glorious emporium.

Otis sadly had to leave to meet Gina at the Cabbage Studios complex, but he vowed that he would be back soon for another vinyl fix.

After being buzzed through security, Otis and Reg were shown to a very modern office, where they were introduced to the production team. Gina left them in the hands of experienced director, Spike Ridley Leigh, who welcomed Otis, and said he would try to contextualise what it was that they were about. He told Otis that Lincolnshire, and Brassica in particular, was a traditional, very steady place, that didn't like any overall dramatic or flashy stuff. Most people seemed to just want to get on with life and not make a fuss. Yes, it was true, he said, that they liked to moan a bit, but that was just most folks' way of coping.

He then asked Otis if he'd heard of a very successful but low-key show from the hill-country up north called *One Man and his Dog*. It started in 1976 and ran for over twenty-three series. In fact, a version of it was still running today. He pressed a button and the show appeared on a large screen which came down from the ceiling. Otis was mesmerised.

'This was on national TV?' he choked, incredulous.

'Had regularly over eight million loyal viewers,' Spike replied. 'It's a great example of what we, in the business, call "slow television". Just like Lincolnshire – nothing flashy, just quiet, rural entertainment with whistling. The only problem was that it wasn't from Lincolnshire.'

Otis was wondering where all this was leading.

'But,' said Spike, 'we are certain that we have finally found our own show to top this one.'

Otis, knowing the Brits' love of animals, wondered what could possibly top a shepherd, his dog, and a small flock of sheep...

Spike said, 'Though we admired *One Man and his Dog*, we wanted something more Lincolnshire, more universal in its appeal, something that touched all our viewers' lives. After all, not many people actually get excited about fencing sheep into small pens, but it still had eight million viewers. Our show has evolved directly from local customs and practices here in Brassica, but connects to people who haven't even seen a sheep in their lives. Our connection is much more universal; literally, much closer to home.' He then focused on Otis and said, 'Otis, no offence, but when did you last wash your clothes?'

Otis felt mortified. Was he giving off some strange odour that he couldn't detect himself? Did he smell? Was his deodorant ineffective? He could feel himself reddening and beginning to panic,

'Serious question,' said Spike. 'We all have to do our laundry – that's the point I'm making.'

Otis certainly didn't feel like going into details about his laundry routine, but he felt sure that what he did was standard practice.

'Our programme, Otis, is about the washing lines of Lincolnshire. Now, I'm sure that such a perceptive person like yourself will understand everybody needs to have their laundry attended to. After all, we're all for the most part, civilised folks these days. Given the universal nature of this domestic activity, we firmly believe that this idea can be franchised around the globe. As you can see, at the Cabbage Corporation, we are keen to stress our organic credentials, so we wish to encourage the traditional Brassica open-air drying techniques. We are totally anti-tumble driers, so wasteful and energy-guzzling. Oh, and we don't tolerate rotary driers on aesthetic grounds.'

Otis was in shock and gazed on, open-mouthed.

Spike pressed on. 'Traditionally, people would go out and look at each other's washing lines. It was something to do to while away the time. They'd say things like "that's a nice line of washing, that is", or "nice pegging", or "level pegging". Sometimes, expressions like "three sheets to the wind" entered the language. A "black line", totally dark clothing, was an unusual sight and therefore worthy of comment. A "total white-out" was usually bedding, and people really appreciated sheets, pillowcases – the full set (with bonus points for a sighting of a rarer valance).'

Spike was in full spate now.

'The activity started as a bit of fun, but then it became a bit more competitive. Local rules started being devised. Some used only wooden pegs, other favoured multi-coloured plastic numbers, but those came to be frowned upon by the environmental fraternity. First it was neighbour versus neighbour, then street versus street, estate versus estate, then village versus village. It was during the recent pandemic that elaborate scoring systems started to be introduced, though to be honest no one really understood the rules, and since they were always "evolving", that wasn't too surprising. It was a bit like those events at the Olympics like skating, dressage, or gymnastics. Literally nobody understands how the scoring works, but they still watch them anyway.

'So, our show has marks for originality, creativity, artistic impression, pegging techniques, colour combinations, et cetera. Wind speed is also taken into account, but you can have too much of a good thing... So popular had this whole activity become, that one particular hot-bed of the craze, the village of Canwick-on-Witham, near Lincoln, had actually changed its name to Washingborough. This was the fervid centre of all things washing-related, the very Wembley, or Wimbledon, of washing.'

Otis was trying to think of anything comparable at home in Alabama – maybe the preaching competitions where ministers vied to be Televangelist of the Year, perhaps?

Spike was inspired. He continued telling Otis how outside radio broadcasts from around the county had been so successful that a TV version was inevitable. He said they had the best minds, creatives, and technical people all working on the show. *Celebrity Washing Lines* was in production; *Whose Washing Line is This?* was also being developed. He said they were also very excited about a show for after the watershed called *Saucy Washing Lines*. Just like the *Real Wives* series, this could go anywhere.

Otis had a strange vision of some of the more unusual washing lines he'd seen in the south after certain menfolk had been to their secret meetings in the woods. When he was a boy, he'd often wondered why grown men liked to dress up like ghosts.

Otis was asked to contribute to a meeting where people were pitching ideas for suitable music to use. *Blowing in the Wind* had a lot of fans, but Cabbage were saying that Bob wanted too much money. *I Walk the Line* was in contention for use when judging started, as was *Blowing Free* by Wishbone Ash. *White Lines* by local Brassica act Gangmaster Flash was vetoed because though *White Lines* had a great intro, it was followed by the words *don't do it* which introduced negative vibes to what was felt to be a bit of light-hearted, wholesome entertainment.

Where the Sheets have No Names by U2 had some supporters, as did Billy Idol's *White Bedding*, but in the end, those were considered too niche. A more all-embracing title was required. In the end, it was the Andy Williams's classic *Music to Wash Clothes By* that won out.

Spike said they were in advanced negotiations with US TV networks, and were deeply encouraged that the word washing appeared prominently in the nation's capital city. A station in Kentucky wanted to know if Cabbage would back their line dancing competition and this was being given serious consideration. Cabbage had passed though on another series idea called *Line of Duty*, saying that nobody could understand what anybody was talking about. Also, it was felt to have no real link to Brassica. After all, Brassica had "Wild Bill" as chief of police, not the Old Bill, and you couldn't get higher than Rob Lowe.

Otis, somewhat shell-shocked, with a face as white as a sheet, eventually got out of there, and suggested to Reg that they go and have a drink at Cultural Mick's before his return to Lincoln.

As Otis drove back to Lincoln, half-thinking of washing lines, he suddenly thought that he'd been so busy dashing all over the county that he hadn't really had the time to explore the city on his doorstep. So, it was to be Lincoln next!

CHAPTER 15

Lincoln Yields Some of its Secrets

Otis woke up to the *Billy Pritchard Breakfast Show* on Radio Brassica. It being food and music month, Billy was interviewing a musicologist from the local University of Lindum about food and environmental influences in The Beatles' catalogue. Professor Vineet Gupta was talking about how The Beatles' trip to see the Maharishi in India had influenced their song-writing. They had, he said, left behind western influences like *Twist and Sprout* and clearly more oriental themes could be detected in their work. He gave the examples of *Okra-di-Okra-da*, *Paperback Raita*, *Baby you're a Rice Man*, and *Curry that Weight*. After playing *Lovely Raita* from the *Sergeant Poppadum* album, Professor Gupta said that those influences carried on in their respective solo projects, too. He cited John and Yoko's *Instant Korma* as a good example.

Billy, another true scion of Brassica, came back and said although those influences were definitely there, they didn't leave more western topics behind. He quoted the very much

Brassica-influenced *Savoy Cabbage Truffle* by George on *The White album*, not forgetting John's *Glass Onion* on the same album. Billy also said that we mustn't overlook John's *Cold Turkey* and the even bigger John and Yoko song *Give Peas a Chance*.

Billy said, 'And while we're on the subject of peas, did you know that Lincolnshire farms produce over one hundred billion peas every year!'

Must be one helluva job counting those, thought Otis.

Professor Gupta accepted very much what Billy was saying. He went on to say that The Beatles' crowning achievement, *Sergeant Poppadum's Curried Pop Tarts Fan Club Band* album, proved this very point with its sublime marriage of oriental and western popular culture.

'In a way,' he concluded, 'this is the very apotheosis of world music in the twentieth century.'

Billy certainly couldn't top that (largely on account of not knowing what apotheosis meant) so he rapidly wound up the interview.

Billy played a song from 1968: *Jesamine*, by Lincoln band The Casuals. Otis was pleased by this as he'd heard from Mary, who was researching Lincoln's musical history that this group used to rehearse in a hut at the end of Boundary Street just off the Newark Road. When it finished, Billy told the listeners how Paul Weller had rated this song as one of his all-time favourites. The song reached number two in the UK chart and number nine in the German chart. For a while The Casuals had worked in Italy, but they returned to the UK to promote *Jesamine* where the new Radio One played it heavily.

Otis made a coffee and then set off to visit the Uphill part of town. He had been told by one of his research assistants to call in to one of Lincoln's hidden gems, a record store called Back to Mono on Guildhall Street. At first, Otis thought it must have moved or closed as he could see a bar, a pub, a coffee shop, a jewellers, a bank and a betting shop, but apparently no record store. A friendly local pointed out that the shop was entered via a pretty nondescript doorway and was located on the first floor. After scaling the staircase, which turned right and then turned right again, Otis was greeted by a fairly large man, Jim Penistan, the owner. Jim was not known for his small talk, but he had an encyclopaedic knowledge of popular music. Otis watched this master at work. In the time he was there, everyone seemed to buy at least one thing, and came away with ideas and suggestions for their next visit. Otis later heard that Jim was also a music promoter, putting on Back to Mono nights in local clubs, and he was also a talented DJ, well respected for his musical taste.

It crossed Otis's mind that he shouldn't have any problem getting hold of records, given that he had a shop full of them. But having the good taste to choose the right records – now, that's what sets the best DJs apart.

Steep Hill was rightly named, he thought, as he wheezed up the hill. Soon, he was standing before the magnificent west front of the cathedral and was amazed by the scale of the whole thing. He caught the end of a guide's explanation about the recently restored carvings on the frieze running the width of the west front.

Evidently, when the carvings were being restored, a sharp-eyed mason noted that in the depiction of Noah's Ark and the flood, all the animals were in pairs except for a lone chimp. This really confused local historians until they found another carving of a chimp high up on an interior pillar near the great east window. Apparently, this cheeky chimp had done a runner! Asking around about this mystery, Otis was told to contact Mick Jones (not the one in The Clash), a local expert who had written extensively about Lincoln's archaeology and history. If Mr English was Mr Gainsborough, then Mr Jones was Mr Lincoln. Mr Jones was away at present, but a friendly cleric provided Otis with a mobile number, so he called him. It was a very bad line, probably the cathedral tower blocking the phone signal. Otis introduced himself and asked his question. From the reply, Otis could decipher something about "digs in London" and "having worked in Grease".

Sounds like a bit of thespian, thought Otis. Anyway, Mick said it had probably been a stonemason with a sense of humour.

Mick said, 'Ask a guide to show you the gargoyles, and you will see what I mean.'

Mick later followed up with an email saying that the Lincoln chimp had become the symbol of the city, with the local soccer team even being called The Chimps UTC.

Next to the cathedral, on its northern side, was the new visitor centre with its beautifully designed garden. Those Poole brothers who were mentioned earlier tried to get the garden named Eden after one of their pop ventures, but the dean was having nothing to do with that.

The castle was next on Otis's agenda; another stupendous structure, complete with towers, portcullis, and battlements! He was impressed to hear that it was sometimes used for musical events. It was a natural amphitheatre, with spectacular views of the floodlit cathedral at night. Otis made a note to find out who had played there.

Otis went into a strange and rather claustrophobic prison chapel where he took the chance to sit down and read the briefing paper that his researchers had provided him with. He noted that in the early 1960s The Beatles and The Rolling Stones had both played in Lincoln at the ABC Cinema, the main venue for concerts in those days. Today it was a bingo club, but all was not lost as the university now had the facilities to host live music.

The local newspaper, *The Lincolnshire Echo*, had printed a series of publicity shots of The Beatles in a pleasure boat on the Brayford Pool. One of the researchers had kindly included a copy of their smiling faces for him to see.

Otis did a little more digging and found that the music scene in Lincoln was not as lively as it used to be. A number of pubs and clubs had closed – for example, the Duke of Wellington pub on Broadgate, which once hosted heavy metal band Saxon in its upstairs room. Now the pub had been turned into a design studio. Generally, there seemed to be fewer venues, especially small ones for young and up-and-coming bands to play in.

Otis was told that the city now hosted an annual Steampunk gathering, but on closer inspection this had nothing to do with music or punk, just a bunch of "peacocks" parading around in bizarre dressing-up clothes and taking pictures of themselves. Very strange. Otis wondered how that would go down back in the Shoals...

Otis was intrigued to hear about something called Barefoot Nights, where a group of like-minded souls got together in local pubs to play and dance to vinyl records. From what he could gather, this was like a collective of RnB and soul music-loving DJs who, for some strange reason, had to play barefoot. He was curious as to how he could get to the bottom of that Lincoln mystery. *Bizarre or what?* thought Otis. The anthropologist in him made him want to attend one of those events and observe the rituals involved. He also thought the Plimsoll Nights at the NALGO club cellar bar sounded interesting, too.

Otis, having finished exploring the castle, found himself outside the cathedral again. He suddenly remembered a strange conversation he had once had with a guy in a used record store on New York's Upper West side. After making small talk, Otis had mentioned his forthcoming trip to Lincoln in the UK.

Quick as a flash, the guy behind the counter said, 'Lincoln? That's near Scunthorpe. That's where my all-time favourite band comes from!'

At the time, Otis had not heard of Scunthorpe so he wasn't aware of quite how strange that observation was. The band, incidentally, was called Amazing Blondel and they played a strangely hypnotic mix of folk, medieval and electric music. Their early albums were released on the cool Island label, home of Free, Fairport Convention, Bob Marley, and Roxy Music.

Otis had been curious enough to seek out some of their albums and he had developed a special liking for Fantasia Lindum, which included a song specially dedicated to Lincoln Cathedral called *Celestial Light*. The band had played the song at a now legendary concert inside the cathedral itself in 1971.

Now that *is some venue to proudly put on the back of your tour t-shirt*, thought Otis.

As he was leaving, he saw a group of tourists staring up at the central tower with binoculars. As he approached them, one of them told him in hushed tones that a pair of green falcon were nesting at the top.

CHAPTER 16

Taking (Vegetable) Stock

A morning in the university's library confirmed Lincolnshire's particular fascination with all things to do with the al fresco drying of clothes. Otis had found two studies in academic journals by Professor Dorothy "Dolly" Tubbe of this very same university. The first, and most interesting paper – *A study of the phenomenon of temporary linear textile installations, and their interactions with the environment and local weather systems* – or *washing lines* – was a masterly exploration of the topic. Otis was hooked.

He read from the abstract:

This contemporary analysis harnesses the latest thinking and developments in ecological and holistic approaches utilising solar and wind power. The engagement of such freely (at the moment) renewable environmental forces, means that it is likely that one could engage repeatedly in this activity, should the need arise. The study concludes that since it is generally considered preferable to wear dry and clean clothing, as opposed to wet and dirty apparel, the benefits are considerable to those who chose to indulge in this traditional activity.

Hm, mused Otis, *there may be more mileage in this washing business than I thought...*

Otis felt it might be useful to meet Professor Tubbe at some point because she, like him, had obviously been out and about working in the field or fields of Lincolnshire. They ought to compare findings. He made a note to bring this up the next time he met with the Head of School who, now he thought about it, had been somewhat quiet for some considerable time. On balance, he thought that could only be construed as a good thing.

At the next team meeting, Otis reviewed the considerable progress that had been made. He also started to compile a list of topics that clearly needed more attention like, for example, Country music. Back home it was everywhere; the soundtrack to everyday life. Here is seemed to only exist in the charity shops he had visited. But, and it was a big but, it existed in enormous quantities. It seemed to him that if all the Country music albums were bulldozed together and buried in a ditch, it might be possible to halt coastal erosion for a hundred years or so. *Was this a generational thing,* he wondered?

A visit was also planned to go back to Brussels Shoals, as so much interesting material had come out of there over the years.

Otis was still coming to grips with the geography of the

watery landscape around Brassica. Lincolnshire, Cambridgeshire and Norfolk all seemed to coalesce and merge and, occasionally, submerge for that matter.

Norfolk seemed very near, but Brassica folk seemed very self-contained and had a somewhat distant approach to their neighbours. Sandringham was quite close by, and sometimes its main resident, for the last three-quarters of a century, used to pop over the county border to carry out royal duties. Otis, in truth being a son of a republic, wasn't quite sure what those entailed. He'd heard a lot of waving was involved, but surely there had to be more to it than that? One time (well, several times actually) Her Majesty the Queen came to open new extensions to the ever-expanding Uptown Vinyl empire. Ever since they'd put that builder, Lennie Annexe, on the payroll, there had been no stopping them. They'd swallowed up Sid's Soft Toys and the Comfort-Fit Casual Slax shop, and they clearly had their eyes on Dave's Half Price but Twice the Pane double-glazing unit.

After giving the royal blessing to extended acres of second-hand vinyl, she visited the Brussels Shoals studio, where Freddie and the boys were recording. She was a big fan, what with the name and all that... Anyway, Fred had this idea for a song, and she joined in on the chorus of *Brassican Rhapsody* – they nailed it in one take! Fred wanted to put it out as Fred and the Boys featuring Lizzie R, but she was having none of it.

'Keep my name out of it, put it out as a Queen single.' She was right too, worked a treat – number one for months on end.

Another area of concern was Grantham – absolutely nothing so far. It was believed there was a statue of Isaac Newton and there was talk of one of a woman, but no sign of it at all.

There was some activity to report from Woodhall Ska, but it needed more research. Evidently, there was one of the oldest cinemas in the country there, and Otis made a note to visit it at some point. Another researcher said that there had been an early rap scene in Brassica, but it needed more work. Otis was hoping to interview a "Gangmaster Flash" very soon. His Boston connection, Toby Carvery, was supposed to be fixing that up, but for some reason those people seemed reluctant to talk on record. Toby had suggested perhaps meeting in Cultural Mick's as a way of starting a conversation. That was fine by Otis; he never minded going there.

Then there was the organic roots music scene versus the more urban feel of Brassica's Stalk 'n' Heads. Their leader, David Byrne-Baby-Byrne (a man named after a pub in Dublin, by the way) was back from touring soon and would be available for interview.

Otis was also curious as to why the Vinyl Triangle was known as such when as far as he could remember without checking his notes, he'd only visited two records stores down in the depths of Brassica. Toby Carvery had told him that some people used to visit a small shop in Market Deeping run from a small cramped room above a barber shop. The word was that it had now closed, or moved to new premises. It had, according to some reports, been rather a gruelling experience trying to buy records there. Nothing was priced, and when you asked how much something was, the guy gazed mysteriously under the counter, played with his keyboard, and then gave you several prices and said "make me an offer" or "let's get creative, let's do a deal". Haggling was all well and good in the souks of North Africa, indeed it was an expected part of the experience, but in a poky little record shop in Market Deeping, well, it just didn't seem right. The simplest of transactions, inevitably, turned into a protracted, embarrassing half-hearted stand-off, when all you wanted to do was hand over cash, get a record and be gone. *Perhaps that's why it closed*, thought Otis. *Perhaps we should refer to the area as the Vinyl Frontier from now on? Either that or find another great record shop down there.*

And what about hip-hop and rap? Surely, they existed in this huge county? Otis asked if there was a file, and he was pleasantly surprised to be offered quite a large folder. There was a sticker on the front cover that read: *Handle with care – contact Brassica Police Department.*

'Woah, what's this all about?' said Otis, pointing to the sticker.

'It's to do with all the gangster stuff. It's nothing, really,' he was reassured.

'Next time I go to Cultural Mick's, I'll check this out.'

After finalising a few items of admin, Otis checked his emails and saw that Daphne Heckington had invited him to appear on her radio show again. It was true that the squirrel trouble seemed to have died down now, but he wasn't too keen to go through all that again. Also, he'd been invited to be a special guest at the Radio Brassica Music and Food Awards ceremony, with the after-party at Cultural Mick's. Now that sounded like fun!

There was a short message from Jack Sabbath or "Old Bolingbroke" as some called him. He said he had some information that Otis might be interested in. He asked Otis to let him know when he'd next be in Cultural Mick's and they could meet up.

It looked like things were pointing to another visit to Boston.

CHAPTER 17

Woodhall Ska "This Town – Looking Like a Golf Town"

As Otis was getting into his pyjamas after another tiring but productive day, he was listening to the late show on Brassica FM. It was Samantha "Smooth" Spridlington's *Brassica All-time Classics Show*. He was so surprised by the haunting opening lines of the song – *This town – looking like a golf town* – that he put both feet into the same trouser leg and proceeded to pogo around the room till he could safely break his fall by crash-landing on the bed. He listened, open-mouthed, till the end of the song, and Samantha didn't disappoint:

'*Golf Town* by Woodhall Ska's very own Specialaka.'

Now this, thought Otis, *is interesting*. He quickly found the file on Woodhall Ska. Evidently, it had started out as Woodhall Spa or rather, going back even earlier, it had started out with a local landowner digging a mineshaft looking for coal. He didn't find any coal and the shaft filled up with water. The water was found to have high concentrations of health-giving substances, so the coalmine turned into a health spa.

Wow, thought Otis. *If Margaret Thatcher had done that, she could have really transformed Britain in the 1980s. Imagine how much lovelier and cleaner the old coalfield areas would have been if all the pithead showers had been converted into luxury spas. Certainly, Grimethorpe would have had to be re-branded, as they say these days...*

It was clear that for some reason the letter K was important here. Otis noticed the 1922 Kinema-in-the-Woods; the Ketwood Hotel, home to the officers of 617 Dambusters Squadron in the Second World War and, of course, the world famous Woodhall Ska Golf Klub. It was believed that K-pop developed out of the tea dances that Buster Bloodvessel started in Ketwood Hotel's splendid ballroom. The girls all wore identical skirts made out of the red and white checked tablecloths (gingham style).

The next morning, armed with a thermos flask of Starbutts coffee and a packet of those brown bourbon biscuits that didn't taste at all like bourbon, Otis was approaching the bridge across the mighty Witham that led into downtown Woodhall. If truth be told, he was still rather shaken having had to avoid the tumbleweed rolling across the main street (possibly the only street?) in Martin, the previous village.

It soon became clear to him that this really was a golf town. He had arranged to go to the famous Ketwood Hotel to meet Major Clipt-Ashe (Rtd) one of the leading authorities on the history of Woodhall.

It was explained to Otis that in 1947 when the natives took

over India again, many British people returned and retired to Woodhall intending to set up "The Golf State of Woodhall Ska". The intention was to set up something exclusive, like the Wentworth Estate in Surrey – a golf course surrounded by luxury homes and villas. Many of them did come, and brought their own servants (the bunker-wallahs) whose job it was to rake the bunkers and roll the greens. As many of the larger houses backed directly onto the course, those people were rarely seen in the town itself and, it's believed, they lived in tents and trailers in the shanty town in the woods. At first, there had been some conflict with the aboriginal Woodhallers who lived and foraged in the woods around the town, but now they lived together in harmony. Their children though were another matter. The locals called them the rude boys and girls, and they tended to have very bad manners and swore a lot. The group lived in the woods and the bad part of town. The words "trailer trash" went through Otis's mind, but he felt guilty immediately for looking down on those less fortunate than himself.

The Woodhall rude boys and girls would, occasionally, appear out of the rough and shout words like bum and arse at people. Sometimes, they would make rude hand gestures too. They tended to reserve the strongest insults for the worst golfers, often shouting bogey or shanker just as they were lining up a serious putt. For the most part, they were tolerated, but sometimes, when they went too far, the klub would send out the Woodhall golf buggy boys with their sprout stalks. The older members called those rude boys and girls spoilt brats, saying they got too much, too young these days.

Otis thought about how some towns back home had divided communities, with those people who lived on the wrong side of the tracks being very much looked down upon. In Woodhall it was easy as they'd got rid of the tracks in 1971, so Woodhall's less fortunate folk lived in the woods, or in some isolated place nearby like Sot's Hole or Tanvats.

In the spirit of anthropological research, Otis wanted to observe this rude boy culture at close quarters. At the Kinema-in the-Woods he was told to send a message to Rudi to try to fix something up. No joy there though, but as he was walking on a path through the woods, he heard the distinctive tone of bluebeat or ska music. He carefully approached and saw a family of the rude tribe at play. They were dancing around a transistor radio. It seemed to be mainly males; large white men wearing pork-pie hats (hats made out of pork pies? One of Lincolnshire's stranger traditions, perhaps) and Crombie coats, running on the spot, elbows bent, with fists pumping up and down in front of their chests.

Not a pretty sight, thought Otis, but he felt deeply privileged to have witnessed this first-hand. It looked like dancing for people who didn't dance. At that moment, Otis stood on a twig, and they all turned and hurled some very rude words in his general direction. Otis beat a hasty retreat, and bought himself a nice ice cream from the pretty and, in truth, pretty old usherette at the Kinema. The Kinema had opened in 1922, and Dolores had worked there most of the time since. It was easier for Dolores to tell you the films that she hadn't seen rather than the ones she had. Otis couldn't resist asking her what her favourite film was. She was torn between several 007 films and *The Guns of Navarone*. It seemed she was a bit of a rude girl, too. She also offered to bite his flake. Once a rude girl, always a rude girl it seemed...

Woodhall certainly had an air of superiority about it. New York City has its Broadway, but Woodhall had "The Broadway". Are they including the definite article to assert the fact that their Broadway was the first and the best Broadway? Probably.

Perhaps the ska scene had taken on some of this sense of superiority. Why else would Terry Hall and his crew call his combo The Specials unless they felt a natural superiority?

Later that day, Otis met up again with Major Clipt-Ashe (Rtd) at his sumptuous ranch-style bungalow overlooking the eighteenth hole of the famous Hotchkin course. The major, or Percy, as he insisted on Otis calling him, said it had recently been voted one of the twenty finest courses in the world. Otis was impressed, even though he could barely tell a wood from an iron.

Percy pointed (with the hand not holding the largest pink gin Otis had ever seen) to a spot near the pin on the eighteenth green.

'That,' he said, 'was where The Selecter got the inspiration for their song *Too Much Pressure*. In a bit of a grudge match with The Specials, Pauline Black developed a serious case of the yips.'

As Percy said, golf could be a cruel mistress; it could really get to you. It could also become a serious addiction. Who knew how many addicts lurked behind the discrete lace curtains of those large houses and bungalows of Woodhall Ska? Of course, that's why many of them moved there in the first place, to be near the source of their greatest pleasure and, ultimately, their greatest frustration. Such was golf.

As the sun was glinting through the trees and casting dappled shadows over the early evening greens, there was a loud rumbling, and a darkness overshadowed the late afternoon light.

'What on earth's that?' said Otis.

'Oh, that'll be Buster Bloodvessel being transported to the nineteenth hole. He has a specially reinforced buggy. Bit of a souped-up engine, but we turn a blind eye.'

As the contraption lumbered past, Otis could hear the subtle, delicate French strains of his wonderful *Can-Can*.

'Such a nice boy,' said the major's good lady wife. 'He runs a choir at the local church, and he played Buttons in last year's Woodhall pantomime. He's the politest person you could meet!'

'Happy days!' said the major as he offered Otis a bowl of the golfer's snack of choice: Pringles.

'Pringle slax and Pringles snax!' quipped Percy. 'What more could a golfer need?'

'We don't eat any of those pedestrian crisps here, thank you very much!'

Otis was looking rather confused, so the major tried to enlighten him.

'The reason we like Pringles, apart from them tasting so good of course, is the fact that they come in sturdy tubes, not those rustly little bags, like inferior crisps. It's the tubes that make the difference. They're so good for putting practice, don't you know?'

Now Otis was really confused, so Percy proceeded to demonstrate with the help of his dear wife, Petunia. In the Astroturfed games and TV room, Petunia was sitting bolt upright, knitting golf club cosies in front of a TV showing re-runs of *The Fresh Prince of Billinghay*. Strategically placed between her elegantly slippered feet was an empty Pringles tube, which the major was in the habit of using for putting practice.

Sheer genius, thought Otis. *These folks are so resourceful, and don't miss a trick.* As golf ball after golf ball pinged unerringly into Petunia's tube (always sour cream and onion flavour, to match the Astroturf), Otis didn't know where to look.

Just at that moment a small, somewhat tubby bunker-wallah emerged silently from behind her chair and smoothly replaced the now full Pringles tube with a fresh empty one, even while the major's latest putt was zipping its way across the carpet. *Such a well-oiled operation*, thought Otis, and come to think of it, not too bad a job either, sitting behind an old lady's chair and scoffing Pringles for all you were worth, with the occasional foray forward to replace her receptacle.

The major told Otis about the klub's latest idea to erect a statue to one of their greatest members, Mr Lee "Scratch" Perry.

'The only player in the klub's history to maintain a zero handicap for the whole of his playing career. A legend in these parts. He used to literally float above the greens, enveloped in a cloud of fragrant aromatic smoke. To be honest, he did go a little strange towards the end. Petunia knitted him a few massive woolly hats – had the whole WI on the job at one time.'

'Actually, we crocheted them,' she said. 'He preferred that look, and it was cooler as the holes aerated his dreads. "Nothing worse than a sweaty scalp", he used to say.'

'Of course – crochet,' smiled the major. 'Got to watch her like a hawk when she gets those hooks out! Incidentally, darling, we'll be needing more bunting soon. I'm told there's another jubilee on the horizon. It's a damned good job we've already got Jubilee Park. Makes things a lot easier. Do you think you could get the ladies' committee on the job?'

'I'll see what I can do when we've finished tonight's practice.'

He then showed Otis a picture of the proposed Lee "Scratch" Perry memorial statue. It was magnificent and so lifelike. The spliff was almost as long as his golf club.

'We gave him a great send off,' said Petunia. 'Buster led the choir and a scratch band called Simply Dread, fresh from their success at this year's Not-In-Hull Carnival, did the honours.'

The major was a big fan of statues and thought we should have more. He said he couldn't abide those namby-pamby woke folk who only wanted to knock them down.

'I'd set the buggy boys on them, make no mistake!'

'You'd set the buggy boys on most people you disagree with,' said Petunia.

Otis felt a little uneasy at the way the conversation had drifted, so he took his leave of the happy couple after strenuously refusing "one for the road".

Otis made noises about not drinking and driving and that set the major off again.

'Couldn't agree more, old chap – one of our klub's more important rules, that. Never drink and drive. That's what the caddy's for: to hold the glass while you tee off!'

Otis noticed a twinkle in the major's eye as he said this, but he was sure that he wasn't joking.

As Otis reached security, he made a point of being on his best behaviour. It always paid to be on the right side of those who wielded the sprout stalks. One of the guys was the driver of Buster Bloodvessel's buggy, and Otis struck up a conversation.

He learned that Buster's real name was Tony Smith, and he and a mate called Tony Brown came out to Woodhall because of the vibrant music scene. The two Tones set up a record label, and the rest is history. Tony Brown, who lived in the Ketwood Hotel, was so obsessed with 617 Squadron, the famous Dambusters, that he changed his name to Jerry Dammers. Together, the two Tones were known round here as Buster Dammers. (It was a little Woodhall Ska in-joke and anyone who didn't get it was sent to Coventry.)

Otis finally took his leave, and started the journey back to Lincoln. As dusk fell, the woods began to reverberate to the competing sound systems which began to crank up at that time of the day. Bluebeat, reggae, ska, dancehall, rock steady – it was all there in the mix.

Otis drove along Station Road. *Funny that*, he thought, *there hasn't been a station here for over half a century. Things move at their own pace in Woodhall Ska.*

Otis thought about a quick drink; just a cola or a club soda in the local pub The Prince Buster, but as he pulled in, he found that it wasn't a pub, but one of those pound shops called Price Buster. Well, anywhere else it would have been a pound shop, but Woodhall being Woodhall the cheapest they would run to were guinea shops. Now Otis was more confused than ever. Still, he managed to buy a cooling can of cabbage cola, despite not being able to locate a guinea in his small change.

As Otis finally drove out of Woodhall Ska, he recalled the words: *Enjoy yourself, it's later than you think...*

How true, he thought, turning a tad melancholy. It had been a long time since he'd been back home in Alabama and for the first time he felt a little homesick. Still, he had plenty of work to do here, and tomorrow it was Boston and Cultural Mick's. He couldn't wait.

CHAPTER 18

Sleaford: No Mods Here

This was the heading of the first email Otis opened the next morning in the office.

Otis had heard of a group called The Sleaford Mods, and given that Sleaford was in Lincolnshire, he felt duty-bound to dig deeper.

It only took about thirty seconds of detailed research courtesy of Mr Google to find that: a) The Sleaford Mods weren't mods, and b) they weren't even from Sleaford.

Evidently they were from Nottingham, which though not very far from Lincolnshire, was most definitely in the neighbouring county of Nottinghamshire.

Robin Hood, the patron saint of Nottingham, paid Lincolnshire a huge compliment by kitting out his merry men in Lincoln green. Otis wasn't sure whether the Sleaford Mods wore Fred Perry shirts or parkas, but since they didn't actually come from Brassica, or even Lincolnshire, he wasn't too minded to find out. Clearly a set of imposters trying to hitch their star to a more successful place.

Another email said that a statue of a woman had been mysteriously helicoptered into Grantham under cover of darkness. This was believed to be the statue of Margaret Thatcher which Westminster Council in London had refused to erect on the grounds that it would be an "incitement to public disorder".

Otis still had no musical reason to explore Grantham, so he didn't anticipate seeing the Iron Lady atop her plinth any time soon.

CHAPTER 19

Boston, Rap and Brat Pack

After sorting out the Sleaford Mods' business, Otis was preparing for his trip to Boston. As he was reading the latest briefing papers from his crack team of researchers, he had a call from Daphne Heckington's PA at Radio Brassica asking him to come on to the show next Friday. She said Daphne was keen to hear how his research was going, and she asked if he would be prepared to talk a little about the food in Alabama. This immediately brought back the feelings of homesickness he had experienced yesterday. It also, more urgently, had triggered pangs of hunger. Oh, for an Alabama breakfast! Not the healthiest of meals, but boy was it good! One of the unwritten rules of the Alabama kitchen was if you can eat it, you can fry it and, in a nutshell, there you have the essence of Alabama cuisine. He was also missing the barbecue and especially the white BBQ sauce that was so popular in his part of northern Alabama.

Otis thought it must be the longest period in his whole life that he'd gone without consuming cornbread, grits and hushpuppies. In the whole time he'd been over in England, he had never ever seen a green tomato, never mind a delicious plate of fried green ones. Now he thought about it, he was sure that someone in the huge food producing area of Brassica could help him out with a little taste of home.

After calling Jack Sabbath to fix up a meeting at Cultural Mick's, he set off for Boston. When he arrived, it was market day and there were stalls all over the market square. Otis asked a woman if they ever sold green tomatoes or okra. She said they never sold okra, but if he really wanted green tomatoes, she thought she could get some from the suppliers. Everyone said they loved the way Otis pronounced tomatoes, and the stallholders were soon all saying tomatoes the way they did in Alabama. Otis said tomatoes had to rhyme with taters, another Alabama favourite, much loved and cooked in Brassica too. This cheered him up to know that it was possible to obtain green tomatoes this far from home.

When he asked about grits he was met with blank expressions all round. It caused much amusement, as people nudged and pointed, not believing that anyone could be so crazy as to eat grit. Otis tried to explain, but it wasn't easy. When he said that it didn't really taste of anything unless you added cheese, or some other flavouring, people thought he must be mad.

Oh well, thought Otis, *it's their loss.*

'What else do you eat back home?' he was asked.

'Biscuits and gravy,' said Otis licking his lips and feeling hungry again.

'No way! Dunking's one thing, but gravy...'

'Crawfish and hushpuppies.'

'You eat hushpuppies? Aren't they a kind of suede shoe?'

Now it was Otis's turn to be confused. 'No,' he said, 'they're a kind of deep-fried corn dough ball.'

'OK, if you say so...'

While it was true that food could bring people together, it was also true that it could show how far apart people could be.

As Otis entered Mick's, he noticed a man standing awkwardly at the bar wearing a wetsuit and flippers.

Jack Sabbath came over, nodded, and said, 'I see you've noticed Clarence over there.'

Otis replied saying, 'You could hardly miss him.'

'That's Clarence "Frogman" Green,' said Jack. 'He works as an underwater diver for BUSTER, the Boston Underwater Supermarket Trolley Eco-Recovery team. These people are on twenty-four-hour standby to ensure the local supermarkets never run out of trolleys, and are seen as a vital cog in the smooth running of the local economy. Being on permanent standby means they can never remove their flippers, so it's a bit awkward when they grab a spot of lunch and Mick's is busy.'

Otis and Jack sat down behind two pints of Boston Bitter, or "Witham Water", as Jack called it.

Jack got straight down to business and said, 'The boss is not well, and it's looking mighty serious and, what's more, if it's terminal, I know for a fact that Simple Dead just won't be able to do that gig.'

Otis was just about to ask for more details on this story, for example, the boss (was that Mick the founder of this hallowed place? Or did he mean someone else?) when the doors burst open and a huge guy walked in, followed by a seriously heavy posse wearing chunky gold chains and fistfuls of large shiny rings.

'That,' said Jack, lowering his voice, 'is the one and only Gangmaster Flash and the Welton Clan.'

'I've been hoping to meet him,' said Otis.

'What on earth for?' said Jack. 'Are you out of your mind? These are dangerous people. Keep well away.'

Just at that moment the door opened again, and someone looking remarkably like the actor Rob Lowe slipped in, followed by several plain-clothed officers.

'That's the local chief of police,' said Jack. 'They always like to keep an eye on Flash whenever he's in town.'

'What's this all about, Jack?'

Jack, not normally a talkative man, leaned in towards Otis and said, 'The gangmasters have traditionally provided a lot of the casual labour force for the seasonal work on the land. The landowners like the system because they don't have to directly employ the workers. So, they deal with the gangmaster who brings in the casual workers on a daily basis, as and when they are required. They often travel from far away and set off well before dawn. They bring them in vans and cram them in, often without seatbelts and no consideration of safety. The gangmasters try to pay the workers as little as possible in order to maximise their own profit. Fall out with a gangmaster, and you'll not get any work. Some of these people are desperate. That's why they endure cramped conditions in overcrowded, rusty vans. The work is often back-breaking, but for many of them there is nothing else.'

Otis had never seen Jack looking so serious. He said, 'So, what's that *white lines – don't do it* song all about, then?'

'That's a song about a network of small rural roads, where they used to drive their ramshackle vans, delivering land workers to the veg and flower fields. The gangmasters used to avoid the main roads, the ones with white lines, as the police tended to wait there trying to catch them, and do spot safety checks. It was very much a game of cat and mouse, or to use a term you'd understand, Otis, it's a bit like the Wild West out there at times.'

Otis appreciated the attempt to make him feel at home, but he didn't like to tell Jack that Alabama was a very long way from the Wild West.

'Gangsta rap, it's believed, originated from gangmaster rap which was the offence of driving cheap farm labour in rusty, overcrowded white vans with no seatbelts.'

Jack pointed over the room and said, 'That's the Welton Clan, but there are many other famous rappers out in this part of Brassica if you know where to look. There's the notorious PIG out Swineshead way; Twenty-Four Carrot in Gedney, a huge man who can hold twenty-four carrots easily in each hand, hell of a worker by all accounts. Then there's Fifty Scents, a flower picker and packer, with a nose so sensitive that he can source the flowers in a bouquet back to the original row in the field.

'Wrap music itself first started in the fruit and veg packing houses, where gangs would wash and pack the produce for the giant supermarkets and high street chains like M&S. These chain-gangs, as they were called, would often sing and chant to while away the hours of monotonous tedium. There are people today who think that monotonous tedium is an apt description of current-day rap music... but each to their own.

'It was Laze-E who first called it rap. He said that the W was a complete waste of space, so he dropped it. He had a serious habit of dropping letters – mainly Es – hence his own name. It was also Laze-E who came up with the term hip-hop one night while waiting for a battered vegan sausage (fried to order) at the local chip shop. He started riffing on the name and now everyone's talking about hip-hop. Some people drop names; he drops letters.

'One guy made a lot of money when he invented double-veg packs. He came to be called Two-Pac. Sadly, he passed away crossing the road at a particularly dangerous junction. Rapping at busy crossroads is especially perilous as some cars drive past very fast indeed.

'Remember Soup Dog? He got a bang on the head crossing the road, and now he keeps forgetting who he is, asking everyone Who am I ?*(What's my name?)*. It's a tragedy, and very boring, as well.'

As Otis was taking in all this new information, he noticed the door open, and a group of what looked like vaguely familiar people walked in and approached the police chief's party. Otis did a double take. 'Surely that's Tom Cruise, Emilio Estevez, Charlie Sheen, Matt Dillon, and Patrick Swayze? Wow, that's nearly a full brat pack!'

'Yeah,' said Jack. 'Ever since Rob Lowe became chief of police, these guys have started turning up for a Friday drinking session. Mick built the helipad out back, but some nights it's still hard to get a parking space.'

There it is again, thought Otis, *another of those special Brassica surprises*. As far as he was aware, those guys weren't in the habit of dropping into the Rocket City Tavern in Huntsville, Alabama for a Friday night drink, but clearly the call of Brassica was hard to refuse.

Otis asked Jack what he knew about the Brassica FM Music and Food Awards, and Jack said it was one of the unmissable highlights of the Brassica calendar.

"A real red-carpet event", were his actual words.

Otis didn't have much call to attend such events in his role of humble Alabama academic, but he thought it sounded like a good idea to hire a tux for the event.

One more drink, a ploughman's lunch, and Otis was on his way back to Lincoln. Oh, how he craved some good ol' Alabama BBQ! The ploughman's lunch wasn't bad but, once again, the ploughman wasn't too happy sharing it with him.

What's so special about these ploughmen? thought Otis. *Why don't they eat normal food like other people? How come they always seem to muscle in on the menu? Plumbers don't do this kind of thing. Might be nice to try a plumber's lunch for a change... Then again, maybe not.*

CHAPTER 20

A Visit to Skegness and the Caravana Coast

The Friday that Otis was booked to appear on the Daphne Heckington show happened to be his birthday. His beloved team of researchers had organised a breakfast team meeting to recap on progress, but what they really intended to do was throw a surprise Alabama breakfast party for their esteemed leader.

On entering the office, Otis was greeted with choruses of "Happy Birthday" and a cacophony of party-poppers that sounded like New Year's Eve in Mobile. He was fêted with sweet potato pie, his favourite fried green tomatoes, boiled peanuts, and biscuits with gravy. The *pièce de résistance* was a magnificent Lane cake – the official state cake of Alabama. The cake was very special (any recipe that started with three hundred millilitres of bourbon had to have something about it). On top was one large volcano of a candle, spitting fire. Otis thought, *if it had been upside down, there was enough power there to put the cake into outer space.* As it was, it only set off the fire alarm.

Later, having consumed a rather large slice of the booze cake, it was time to go to *The Daphne Heckington Show*. Otis had been expecting to go to the studio in Uphill Lincoln, but he had learned that this week the show was being broadcast live from a sound stage on the beach, at Lincolnshire's premier seaside resort of Skegness. This would be a first for Otis. In his travels around the county, he had often heard the locals talk of the coastal strip of Caravana, and jokingly refer to Skeg Vegas. Now he would see it for himself.

He noticed the statue of The Jolly Fisherman gambolling along in a pair of large Wellington boots. It was said that holidaymakers from Nottinghamshire and Leicestershire often arrived wearing similar wellies as they rapidly raced to unpack, and rushed, hot-footing it to the gaming arcades and slots hoping, literally, to fill their boots.

Skeg was different to the rest of the county; no doubt about it. Groups of people shuffled up and down along the sea-front having a good time. The people seemed to Otis to lack a spark, and then he hit on a possible answer. Out at sea was a forest of whirring wind turbines and those seemed to have a hypnotic effect on most people. It wasn't that they were zombies: they'd simply been hypnotised by staring out to sea. That had to account for the totally chilled out state of most folks there.

Otis noticed a poster for the Embassy Theatre in Skegness and he wondered who had performed there. He must remember to ask Daphne later.

He soon found the Radio Brassica sound stage as it had attracted quite a crowd on the beach. The crowd were not very animated, it had to be said, then Otis realised that most of them were staring out to sea and had come under the spell of the mysterious wind turbines. Red-coated youngsters were giving out Radio Brassica buckets and spades as Lulu's big '60s hit *Sprout* blared out across the sands. Otis was taken to Daphne's inner sanctum and handed a Radio Brassica mug of steaming Bovril. It sure was bracing out there on the coast. Daphne greeted him like a long-lost friend and gave him a kiss on both cheeks. She said she would ask him about how his work in the county was going, and she wanted to explore how he was finding the local food, and how it compared to the stuff he was used to back home.

Otis felt he could take all that in his stride, but wondered whether the beach zombies would be at all interested. He told himself, *keep it short and light-hearted, and definitely no squirrels this time...*

After playing *Patches* by fellow Alabama resident Clarence Carter, Daphne welcomed Otis on to the stage, and the broadcast interview started.

'Welcome again to Professor Otis K Spanner III, who is visiting us for a year, researching the rich musical history of Brassica.'

'Good to be here again, Daphne, and great to see y'all again! And thanks for playing a song by my fellow Alabaman,

Clarence Carter. He sure is one of the last of the old-style Southern soul men!'

'So, Otis, how is the work going?'

'Much better than I'd ever anticipated. This place has a rich and varied musical history. It's constantly throwing up surprises. I never knew it was so seminal and influential. There are surprises and great finds in every part of Lincolnshire, and especially in Brassica, to the south.'

'Well, that's great to hear, Otis. Will you be publishing your findings in book form so we can all read it and share in your discoveries?'

'Well, Daphne, that is the intention, but there's a lot of work to be done before it will hit the bookstores!'

'Well, good luck with that, Otis, we'll look forward to it – be sure to let us know when you have a publication date.'

'I sure will, Daphne, make no mistake!'

'Now, you've been here several months. How are you finding life here? Are you homesick? How're you finding the food here? I guess it's very different to Alabama chow.'

'The time has flown past so quickly I've hardly had time to feel homesick. I must admit, I have missed home cooking, but even this morning I had a little taste of home, courtesy of my fellow workers at the university who surprised me with some Alabama treats.'

Daphne's eyes lit up and she said, 'We have a surprise for you, too! A little bird told me it was your birthday and so we've made you a cake!'

A huge Lane cake was wheeled onto the stage as Daphne led the assembled beach crowd in a somewhat disjointed version of *Happy Birthday*.

Otis was touched by the gesture and was overcome with emotion. As the Radio Brassica redcoats handed out pieces of the booze-fuelled cake, half of the hypnotised crowd were overcome with fumes and could be seen rushing wildly into the brown North Sea.

Otis stayed around and talked to Daphne while the records were spinning. He asked her about the Embassy Theatre and she said that Ken Dodd had played there over three hundred times. This wasn't a name that was familiar to Otis (clearly the bard of Knotty Ash had not reached across the ocean and impacted on Alabama. His tickling stick was long, but not that long).

Daphne said that Ken Dodd had recorded the UK's third biggest selling single in the whole of the '60s.

'But The Beatles, The Stones – more than all those great bands?'

'Well, The Beatles had the top two biggest sellers, *She Loves You* and *I Wanna Hold Your Hand*, but Ken Dodds's *Tears* outsold all the rest.'

'Well, you learn something new every day,' said Otis.

'Well, here's another new thing for you. Since we're talking about Skegness and The Beatles...'

'Don't tell me they played here as well?'

'Well, not all of them. Ringo played here in 1962 with Rory

Storm and the Hurricanes, a Liverpool band that had a summer residency in the town. John Lennon and Paul McCartney allegedly made the long cross-country journey to head-hunt Ringo for the band. Quite a successful trip for all concerned, really.'

Otis thanked her for the kind gesture of the birthday cake, and asked her what role she had in the forthcoming awards show. Daphne said she was an executive producer and she would be sharing some introductory duties with some other presenters. Some had suggested bringing back the legendary Alan Cartridge, doyen of Lincolnshire radio, who despite his recent troubles was still popular with the public.

Cartridge was most famous for breaking Jeremy Paxman's record of asking an interviewee (Michael Howard) the same question twelve times. Paxman never received an answer. It was the annual search for the county's favourite sausage roll and Cartridge had been sent out into Lincoln on a vox pop mission. In Sincil Street, outside FW Pepperdine's esteemed butcher's shop, he encountered a butcher who always seemed to be standing in front of the shop. Fifteen times he asked him what the special ingredient was that made Pepperdine's sausage rolls so desirable. Alan never received an answer, but channelling his inner Paxman, he'd ploughed on regardless. It was only late in the afternoon when two employees came out and lifted the butcher back inside the shop that he realised the error of his ways. The life-like statue, a local landmark, had stood there for generations, signalling that the shop was open for business. He blamed stress, having had to sample far too many sausage rolls in too short a space of time, overwork, and having put his contact lenses in back to front. Eye-witnesses, or should that be nose-witnesses, claimed that there was definitely a strong smell of alcohol on his breath. Fortunately for him, being a pedestrian in a pedestrian zone, he managed to avoid being breathalysed. Alan claimed that it was overuse of his trademark aftershave that had caused that misunderstanding. Sadly for him his bosses disagreed and Cartridge was fired. They also removed all evidence of the somewhat one-sided interview from all social media platforms which Otis thought was a great pity. After several months in rehab for his sausage roll addiction, he had slowly rebuilt his career and had moved on to other, bigger things, and was currently away filming an advert for Athlete's Foot cream in Scunthorpe.

Daphne said she always stayed over in the Brassica Five Seasons Hotel in Boston, and she said to Otis that he ought to do the same. He said that he'd get on to it right away.

Two slices of Lane cake in one day was enough to stop an elephant in its tracks, but fortunately Otis was made of sterner stuff.

CHAPTER 21

Stamford Punk Central

Otis had driven home very carefully from Skegness as he didn't want to have the dubious honour of being the first person in the UK to be breathalysed for eating too much cake.

As was now usual practice, he sifted through his emails, metaphorically screwing most of them up and lobbing them into the great electronic dustbin in the sky. One email did catch his eye as it was written in what looked like cut-out letters from a newspaper, a bit like a ransom note, or the Sex Pistols's album cover.

It read: *Prof Spanner, we need to talk about Stamford. Yours, Cecil*. Under the single worded name were some contact details.

Otis found a copy of the county map and found Stamford at the southernmost point of the county, almost in Cambridgeshire, or Rutland, or Leicestershire, for that matter. Otis was curious about the email, so he took the liberty of calling the mobile number appended.

A rather superior-sounding voice finally answered, saying, 'To whom do I have the pleasure of speaking?'

Otis briefly explained that he was replying to the somewhat enigmatic email from Cecil and wanted to know why he had been contacted.

'Ah, yes, you must be Professor Spanner. Please forgive my being so bold as to contact you in this way, but it has come to my attention that you are conducting some kind of survey or research into the musical heritage of Lincolnshire, and I feel it imperative that you learn something about Stamford and its role as Lincolnshire punk central in the late 1970s. I might add that this is not my particular bucket of spittle, but as something of an amateur local historian I do like to set the record straight.'

Otis now recalled a team meeting where someone had mentioned Stamford as a possible place to visit. He had asked why, but no real answer had been forthcoming. Now perhaps be would find out more.

He'd also been told that Stamford was posh. So posh in fact that the locals didn't feel they really belonged to Lincolnshire at all. If little neighbour Rutland could be a county, then Stamford felt it should be a county too. People in Woodhall Ska thought they were posh, but true Stamfordians thought Woodhall was nothing better than a gutter on the edge of Horncastle.

Cecil explained that he wasn't one of the Cecil's from the big house of Burghley, on the edge of town. He said that

Stamford was like a little bit of the Cotswolds that had, for some inexplicable reason, drifted northeast over thousands of years, and ended up just north of Peterborough. Cecil said Stamford had started out as Burghley House's backyard, and it was said that those in the know in the town always christened their first-born son Cecil because that name seemed to open doors all over town.

Stamford, having an unusually large number of posh kids, for some reason became a hot bed of punk music. It was a combination of extraordinarily long, boring holidays back from boarding school, oodles of money, and absolutely no musical talent whatsoever. A truly winning combination.

Some of the great inspirations and punk heroes went to some of the finest private schools: Shane McGowan, Westminster; Joe Strummer, a boarder for seven years at the City of London Freeman's School in Surrey; Johnny Putrid, Eton, and Sid Viscous, Harrow. Clearly all hot beds of anarchy and rebellion.

Cecil explained that toffs had time and they had money, so they could buy the best equipment for their little darlings who could afford to smash it up because Daddy would always shell out more to keep them sweet, and at arms' length.

'Stamford became a magnet for rich kids, especially at the start of the long summer holidays. Some of them were spectacularly devoid of talent and should have gone far, but I suppose it all depends who else is in the band and how the chemistry works. That Rees-Mogg chap from Eton auditioned for Cham 69 because he said his papa had said that was a very good vintage. He never made it, of course, though he did stand in for Bez in The Happy Mondays a few times. Another Etonian, that blond kid who thought he just had to mess up his hair and he'd be top dog, he never made it, either. He later entered Eurovision, scored "nul points" and then tried to tell everybody that he'd actually won! He now maintains that we will have to wait for the report to find out whether he actually even entered the contest in the first place, that is the contest that he still claims he actually won fair and square.'

You couldn't make it up, thought Otis. *Surely, nobody could take this joker seriously?*

Cecil said to Otis that if he did find time to visit Stamford, not to forget to visit the Mosh Pit, the home of Snotify, the very successful punk streaming service based in the town.

Otis thanked Cecil and said it had been a really useful conversation that had filled a serious gap in the county's musical history.

Before finally signing off, Cecil invited Otis to visit the Burghley Hoarse Trials later in the year. This was an annual competition where punk bands, and latterly thrash metal bands from Rutland, had competed to see who could scream longest and loudest. The Banshees had a great record to defend, but they couldn't keep it up like they used to, so there may be a new champion soon.

Getting back to Snotify, Otis thought, *I suppose I could download the app...* But in truth this just wasn't his cup of tea (or bucket of vomit, or whatever punk term was currently appropriate).

Well, he had to get on, the big show was approaching fast, and there was much work to be done, and he couldn't let the grass grow under his feet. After all, it was the great Joe Strimmer who had sung *I fought the lawn and the lawn won*.

Not on my watch, thought Otis.

CHAPTER 22

Getting Ready for the Big Show and a Shock

The next time Otis saw Daphne was the day before the grand awards ceremony. Otis had managed to obtain one of the last rooms in the Boston Brassica Five Seasons Hotel. Daphne had asked him to come up to her suite as she wanted to run through with him his small, but significant part, in the night's proceedings. Being a distinguished foreign visitor to those shores, he had been asked to present the award for the best foreign song; foreign referring in this instance to areas outside but neighbouring Lincolnshire and Brassica. There were four contenders this year, though as ever with these things, one of the choices was controversial. Daphne loved a bit of controversy, she said. It kept the listeners on their toes.

'Listeners?' said Otis. 'I thought this was being televised?'

'Oh, it is,' said Daphne. 'Cabbage Studios are streaming it live around the world. I said listeners through sheer force of habit. I started, and I'll end my days, on Radio Brassica!'

'Well, what's the iffy one?' asked Otis.

'It's Woodhall Ska's Specialaka's song *Free Nelson's Mam Ella*. You see, we originally included it because everyone knows Nelson was from Norfolk, and of course Norfolk borders Brassica to the south.'

'I think you're on thin ice, there,' said Otis.

Daphne replied, 'Don't worry, it's not going to win – we've already decided who's going to get the award.'

'And do you mind telling me?' said Otis. 'No, wait a minute. Who are the other contenders?'

'There's *Thorne in my Side* from South Yorkshire, *Trent Town Rock* from Nottinghamshire, and finally my favourite by Stalk 'n' Heads, *Hedon (a place where nothing ever happens)* from East Yorkshire/Humberside.'

'That's a great song,' agreed Otis. 'I take it that's the winner, since you said it was your favourite?'

'Well, I do have a certain influence around here,' smiled Daphne. 'All you have to do is announce the contenders and open the envelope!'

'I think I can just about manage that,' said Otis, smiling back.

Otis looked around the room and saw that it resembled what he assumed a war operations room would look like. There was a huge paper plan of the Starlight Rooms and the arrangement of tables ready for tomorrow evening. There were many additions and deletions and arrows indicating that certain individuals had to be moved on account of past indiscretions and rivalries.

'What does all this mean?' said Otis.

'Let's just say that we've learnt from past experience that a lot of thought has to go into seating plans – we don't want to put Oasis next to Blur again. Or, Liam next to Noel, come to that... Or Liam on his own, come to think of it...'

Otis didn't get the details but he understood the gist.

Daphne said many important guests had agreed to attend and some were being given special awards. She also said it was important to look after the corporate sponsors as they made the whole show possible. This was a unique event, given Brassica's pre-eminence in the food and music industries. It had been a masterstroke to combine those two specialist strengths of the area together.

'After all,' she said, 'the Oscars only deal with movies, but we deal with two hugely important areas of human experience.'

She ran through the running order from the top, starting with the Fentastic Four's *Tribute to Brassica: a musical celebration of veg from asparagus to zucchini*. (Not that ninety-nine per cent of locals would know what zucchini was. Let's be fair, a good eighty-five per cent wouldn't know a courgette if it was waved in front of their faces. Not that that was a likely event in Lincolnshire as most people were coy when it came to talking openly about veg. It was just not done to flaunt that kind of stuff in public).

Next up, Toyah was to introduce Diana Roth, singing *I'm Coming Sprout*. Then Diana was to introduce local crooner,

Nat King Coleby, singing about a woman, *Moaner Lisa*, who complained about everyone in that charming cliff-edge village. Then, it was on to the presentations. Between each award, there was to be a performance by an act with particular significance to the Brassica region. Daphne's job was to hold the whole thing together.

Otis was beginning to get a sense of how big this entire event was. Daphne told him that a whole crew of Michelin-starred chefs were already hard at work with their talented knife-wielding teams, transforming the exceptional Brassica produce into five-star finger fodder for the big night tomorrow.

As Otis walked across town to check out the Starlight Rooms, he suddenly felt the buzz. The centre of town was busy with workmen erecting marquees, and creating roped-off VIP zones wherever possible. There were pop-up shops popping up everywhere; Tiffany's, next to the Lithuanian food market, Versace next to Cash Converters, and Mappin and Webb, around the corner from the food bank.

Mappin and Webb, the royal jewellers, had strong local connections as co-founder, Robert Webb, was born in Horncastle. He of course went on to team up with Davey Mitchell from Mitchell and Butlers, the brewing dynasty, to set up Mitchell and Webb, official off-licence and jewellery store to HM The Queen Mother. Staff there loved to reminisce about her frequent visits – it was always "two bottles of Dubonnet, a bottle of brown, four cans of Irn Brun, a diamond tiara and a bag of pork scratchings". God rest her soul.

Harvey Nicks had drafted in staff from their Baytree garden centre concession, and had taken over a couple of corner shops near the football ground. Suddenly, it seemed that all the minicabs had turned overnight into stretch limos. A pop-up shop called White Stuff opened near Pump Square, and police chief Rob Lowe immediately sent in the sniffer dog squad. They evidently took away several duvet covers and a couple of pillowcases full of "talcum powder". Quite a result for the still relatively new other American import into Brassica.

The legendary DyslexicKaraoke Crew had opened one of their famous pop-up stores selling their classic dyslexickaraoke t-shirts. The Who seemed to have inspired some of this year's favourites; *I Can See Four Miles* evidently being a big seller to folks from the Gedney Hill part of Brassica. *Magic Bust* was another popular female line. But nothing could get near this year's runaway Brassica bestseller, *(Talking 'bout) My Generator*.

As Otis turned a corner he was shocked by a sign along the street: *Daily Sex Institute*.

Well, that's a bit blatant, he thought. *Hamburg's Reeperbahn maybe, Soho, definitely, but surely not in Boston, Brassica?* At that movement, a man in dark glasses emerged and walked towards him.

Otis couldn't resist approaching him and he said, 'Excuse me, sir, but what exactly is this place?'

The man looked embarrassed and pointed to the sign, 'Can't you read? It says Dyslexia Institute. All reading problems addressed. I've been going there for years. They gave me these special glasses, and now I can read letters I couldn't even see before. Marvellous place!'

Otis looked at the sign again and to him it definitely read *Daily Sex Institute*, but clearly others saw it differently.

There were also a lot more tourists than usual. Otis had heard earlier about Lincoln Steampunk Weekend, when people dressed up and paraded round town in fancy and fanciful costumes. Here, Otis kept seeing people and characters he thought he recognised. His old friend Reg Carvery explained what was going on. It was something called "cosplay", not a word he was familiar with, so he'd had to look it up.

Cosplay: the practice of dressing up as a character from a film, book or video game. That explained the two Darth Vaders he'd just seen walking out with their light sabres. Reg also said that George Lucas had originally taken the idea for the light sabres from the original Brassica sprout stalk, but he'd been careful not to say too much on account of copyright.

Reg also explained another thing that had been puzzling Otis, about the number of people walking around dressed as lettuces. Reg said there was a strict orthodox Brassica sect that interpreted cosplay as only referring to lettuce, hence their rather strange outfits.

'It all adds to the gaiety of nations,' said Otis.

Reg gave him a funny look and said he didn't think it involved any of that kind of stuff.

Otis was feeling excited, nervous, and somewhat privileged to be part of this great occasion.

He'd heard that a number of blues musicians had checked in to the Fishtoft Crossroads Motel, and there was to be a guest appearance of a blues duo from nearby windy Norfolk: Mr Buddy Guy and Junior Wells-next-the-Sea. The word on the street was that the Robert Crayfish Band might also appear. Otis was hoping to catch them later.

It was just at that point that he took the phone call from Daphne that changed his mood completely. The Boss was dead. Mr Bruce Spring-Green, musical legend of these parts, was no more.

CHAPTER 23

Missing the Boss

Otis rushed back to his hotel room, barely able to take in the news. He immediately switched on the local TV news and he caught a guy from Hull Hospital Radio, a Peter Underscore-Lily, talking about the demise of the Boss.

He said, 'The death of Fenland rock legend, Bruce Spring-Green, has just been announced. He was probably the most important artist to come out of Brassica – ever. They say it was the Ouse that killed him. He'd always had a taste for it. He was addicted to wild swimming, and it's believed he drank too much polluted river water and drowned. His song *The River* about the very same Great Ouse (the river that crime writer, Raymond Chandler, called The Big Seep) will be a fitting, and perhaps macabre testament to a great career. They found his body in The Wash. Like everything around here, it all comes out in The Wash.'

Otis felt a tear come into the corner of his eye. He then remembered Jack Sabbath's comment that Simply Dead would not be able to play him out. Surely a wake for the Boss, without music, would be unthinkable?

The TV coverage then went over to Brussels Shoals and another announcer took up the story.

'Bruce's career had its ups and downs. The highs had to be the series of legendary live shows at the East of England Showground, just off the A1 near Peterborough. He broke all attendance records; the only artist to attract crowds bigger than the annual Monster Trucks festival. Amazing!

'The low point has to be having to settle all those claims brought against him by those people who'd had accidents, dancing in the dark: broken hips, legs, twisted ankles, the lot. After that, the CD could only be sold with prominent health warning stickers attached.

'The worst setback was the caravan park disaster at Hashberry Park, Ingoldmells in 1999, when that chap knocked over the paraffin heater and took out seventeen static caravans. The judge's summing up stated that all the evidence proved conclusively that you most definitely can start a fire when dancing in the dark.

'After that, Bruce had had to go to the big city of Lincoln to get his career back on track. He took on a residency working on the river boats (he always had an attraction to water). The candlelit cabbage cruises on the *Brayford Belle* became a regular, if not exactly lucrative, earner. It was a long way from the East of England Showground – about fifty-five miles.

'Amid all the eulogies to this hard-working local hero, there was considerable concern for his colleagues in the E-Stream Band. They were never the sharpest of minds, but boy, could they play. Who can forget Bruce's story about the first time they played in New York? (The one in the US, not the one near Coningsby, in Lincolnshire.)

'While Bruce was doing media interviews before the Madison Square Garden opening, the band instructed Vince and Len, their loyal and long-suffering roadies, to set up their gear in the garden in Madison Square. Two hours before the show was supposed to start, the NYPD moved them on, and they made the gig just in time. The drummer, Jethro, the brains of the band, still says how were they to know that Madison Square Garden was not actually in Madison Square. I suppose he has a point. He said, "In Lincoln, Boultham Park is in Boultham", which of course is very true. Without Bruce, how could they carry on?'

Otis called Daphne to see how she was taking the news.

Daphne was red-eyed and snuffling, but said, 'The show must go on!'

What a trooper, thought Otis. He asked her if she'd eaten yet, and she said only finger food. One of the hottest young French celebrity chefs kept sending up little trays of cabbage in choux pastry.

'But doesn't "choux" mean cabbage in French?' asked Otis. 'So, he's serving you cabbage in cabbage pastry?'

'I guess so,' said Daphne. 'I've never thought of it like that. Anyway, it tastes delicious. You have to remember, Otis, I'm a

Brassica girl, born and bred!'

Otis said he'd come over, but would get some food of his own on the way.

The town was heaving with people. It reminded Otis of the time he'd visited Austin in Texas during the SXSW festival. There was music coming out of every doorway, TV crews lining the streets, and people being interviewed on every street corner.

When he finally fought his way up to Daphne's suite, she told him that they'd had to drastically revise tomorrow night's show. Only the most important awards were being presented on the show; the others would be announced at a later date.

Most promising newcomer, suitably sponsored by the parish council of Great Gonerby, the aptly-named village just outside Grantham, had already been announced on Brassica FM a few minutes ago; Horncastle band Anyone for Tennyson?'s creative rap re-interpretations of the local poet's greatest hits, the worthy winner.

She asked Otis to be at rehearsal at ten a.m. sharp the next morning. Otis was impressed with Daphne's efficiency and utter professionalism. He had to admit that he had a growing admiration for her...

Daphne was in overdrive, rewriting schedules and re-scripting introductions, so Otis took his leave to see if he could catch The Robert Crayfish Band who were playing in one of the many Witham 'n' blues clubs in the town. By the time he got there it was dark, but he wasn't afraid of it.

CHAPTER 24

Rehearsal: Show Time Minus One

As Otis went down for breakfast at the Five Seasons, he was amazed at the range of food: eggs scrambled, boiled, sunny side up, eggs over easy, omelettes, even huevos rancheros. But still no grits. He asked the waitress about the hotel's unusual name and she said it referred to the usual four seasons, and the hotel's aim to provide a permanent season of goodwill!

She then bobbed, and said, 'Have a nice day!'

Thinking about the Boss's untimely departure, he said that he sure would try.

The dining room was host to a startling number of famous faces, all of course with local connections, back in town for the big show that night. At the table near the window was Mr Jim Broadbent, fresh from his Best Supporting Actor Role Oscar, where he played a vase in the flower bio-pic *Iris*. Otis felt the urge to go over and tell him what an ornamental performance that had been. He also wanted to ask him how had he managed to keep still for so long? *Method acting, I suppose*, thought Otis.

Though he was a huge fan, Otis felt too inhibited to actually approach the great actor, and to be brutally honest Otis preferred his earlier National Theatre of Brent work, if truth be told. He also recognised the actor John Hurt, who'd evidently spent his formative schooldays in Lincoln. It was John who surprised us all when his stomach burst open in the movie *Alien*, giving birth to a monster of a child. That film had been one of the biggest grossing (and grossest) movies of all time, largely because it had been licensed to many of the Southern US states as part of their sex education programs. The longer Otis stared at him, the more he remembered that day in junior high school, when most of the girls had fainted, and sworn blind that they'd never go near a boy again.

It was a little-known fact that certain later scenes from John's other classic *The Elephant Man* were used in several Alabama counties to warn young boys what would happen to you if you committed the sin of Onan. *Talk about shock therapy*, thought Otis.

Over by the vegan bar, Joaquin Phoenix-Nights was loading up on tofu snacks. He'd recently been in the county filming Spike Scott Ridley-Leigh's new show about Napoleon, working title: *Pas Ce Soir, Josephine*. This show was co-produced for Cabbage TV by Woodhall Ska funnyman, Peter K.

After a last frozen kale custard yoghurt, Otis tiptoed out of the presence of greatness and set off on the short walk to the morning rehearsal.

As he'd expected, Daphne ruled the proceedings with, if not a rod of iron, then a large sprout stalk. At times, she would bang a huge gong in order to get everyone's attention.

The Fentastic Four were to open the show with their *Tribute to Brussels Shoals*.

Brian Eno was on board producing the incidental, ambient music. There was no other choice, given his wonderful soundtrack for the *Spring Watch* lambing sequence. Sheer genius, from a master at the top of his game. Some say that he invented the sub-genre of 'lambient' music

The first award, the I'll Eat Anything, But I Won't Eat That Meatloaf Memorial Award, had four contenders: Robert Plant, Bruce Spring-Green, Suzanne Vegan, and Pak Choi, for his contribution to Special K-pop.

In the circumstances, Bruce was being given the award, and Robert Plant was to collect it, and pay tribute to the great man.

After Frankie Knuckles had performed one of his inimitable Burghley House music tracks, it was on to the next presentation. It was the Furrow and Gall Artist of Colour award.

At one time, this had been quite a controversial topic, attracting protests and rallies in villages all over Brassica. But giving the first award to Barry White had been a masterstroke on Daphne's part, and all protest died down. Subsequent winners like Pink Floyd, Black Sabbath, Deacon Blue, and Deep Purple showed how prestigious the award really was. Woodhall Ska's Pauline Black was to present the award. This year's contenders were: Red Sheeran, Green Day, David Gray, and the Red Hot Chili Peppers. It was known that Flea had flown in yesterday, so it looked odds on that the Peppers would be winning that one.

Next up, a specially re-formed Vegetable Underground, performing their own brand of Brassica roots music, *Sweet Kale*. Daphne stopped them mid-tune and asked the singer Blue Reed to smile a bit more. He was not happy, and ended up gurning like Iggy Pop. Rock 'n' roll attitude was what Otis put it down to. Otis didn't like the way Reed glared at Daphne.

It was the turn of the food sector to get a look in. The next award, sponsored by the peerless Bardney Bakery, was The Most Innovative Sandwich of the Year. It was to be presented this year by David Gates, the driving force behind super group, Bread. As a nod to the currently fashionable diversity lobby, this category had been widened to include brown and white bread, together with baps, rolls, cobs, bagels, and even this year baguettes! People still talked, in hushed, awed tones, about the very first winner, the Jelly Roll Morton. Yep, a dessert sandwich.

This year's contenders included a few curveballs: The Chattanooga Choux-Choux – yellow cornbread double cabbage (red and white), doused in a Tennessee bourbon blueberry sauce. *Very patriotic*, thought Otis. The Wigtoft Steak and Kidney Pie Sandwich, served in a baguette, on a bed of shredded slaw; The Bacon Sandwich, served on lightly buttered Mother's Pride, and finally, the real curveball, the

Dominic's Pizza Cheese-Filled Trouser-Turn-Ups for snacks on the go. Even though this was only a rehearsal, people were protesting and shouting "cheat"! and "that's not a sandwich"!

Otis had a feeling that the simple genius of the bacon sandwich had caught the mood, and was going to run away with the prize. A table reserved for Mother's Pride executives tended to suggest he had guessed correctly.

After this award, Daphne announced that there would be a live tribute to the Boss beamed in by satellite direct from Dollywood, Tennessee. The Dolly Parton sisters (you may remember that Dolly was the first Country Music star to be cloned, so she could double her earnings) or The Dollies, as they are now universally known, would pay tribute to Bruce, the great blue-collar superstar, by singing one of his songs. The producer had vetoed the first choice *I'm on Fire*, given the caravan park disaster, so they ended up choosing *The River*.

Given Bruce's passion for wild swimming, Daphne predicted that there wouldn't be a dry eye in the house.

Otis ran through the best foreign song category that Daphne had told him about yesterday. He'd felt a little self-conscious, but he got through it without a hitch.

The last thing to rehearse was the grand finale. It was to have been the Haven Hookers doing a big production number of the old Edwin Hawkins's song, *Oh Happy Day*. But what with the Boss's demise, it was decided to choose a more suitably downbeat tune. The Haven Hookers incidentally had started out as a fishing club for those Brassica women who spent too much time hanging around the docks.

When Mad Donna, the material girl from Boston market joined, they started singing, and had never looked back. The group's composition was not fixed, as girls sometimes have to spend periods of time away.

'I suppose it's more like a cooperative, really,' said Daphne, trying to explain to Otis who those girls were.

Local Brassica producer, Booker T-Bone Steak, had been given the task of arranging this last *pièce de résistance*. Booker T, a local legend, started out working at the Spalding cash and carry. He was a real organic musician – Brassica through and through. He'd had a few food-related hits of his own in his early years: *Green Onions*, *Red Beans and Rice*, and *Chip-Hug-Her*. Otis thought that maybe he'd been hungry as a child.

When the Hookers took to the stage, they were a somewhat intimidating presence. It was hard to believe so much talent could actually fit on one small stage. There was Mad-Donna, Karen Carp, Ronnie Baitt, Carole King-Prawn, Tailor Swift, Kate Thrush, Katie Tongue-Stud, Gedney Houston, Sonny-Ann Share, Rita Oreo, and Aimless Melissa the Anagram Queen. Otis was impressed, but Booker T shouted, 'Where are the rest of the girls?'

Evidently, at full strength, there were seventeen in all, hence the nickname Haven 17. Temptation with a capital T!

At that moment, the three final pieces of the jigsaw turned up: Yvonne Fair, Bette Middling, and Tina "Simply the Best".

Wow, thought Otis, *I think I'll stick around for a while.*

After a wonderful acapella version of *A Whiter Shade of Kale*, Daphne said everything was ready for tonight.

As people were arranging limos to take the stars back to their hotels, Otis gathered that many were staying in the isolation unit of Pilgrim Hospital which, he was told, was converted every year into a luxurious hotel to house the influx of stars and media folk to this prestigious event. The avoidance of in-house catering evidently added to its appeal as the Cabbage Corporation provided top-class chefs to create a bottomless buffet of Brassica classics.

Heavy metal bands took over A&E for the night, some saying it was just like the Grammys, or the Oscars, what with all the waiting around, but in fact it was considered generally quieter than a usual Friday or Saturday night in Boston.

For many years there'd always been a rumour that David Bowie would show up, especially as his scheduled gig at the Gliderdrome had been cancelled due to its unforeseen closure. David was playing at being Ziggy then. It was a little-known fact that he was originally going to be called Zippy Stardust, after a character in *Rainbow*, a kids' show on TV in the early '70s. Zippy was unique, like David; he bore no obvious resemblance to any real animal. Presenter Geoffrey Hayes said: "I don't think anyone has a clue what he's meant to be". He was talking about Zippy, not David or Ziggy, but he could have been... Anyway, Zippy blew David out of the water and, pretty soon, David killed Ziggy off. This obviously disturbed David, because he could never settle and always seemed to be changing. How unlike the other great British superstar, Cliff. You somehow always knew where you were with Cliff.

As Otis walked back across town, he bumped into Richard Ashcroft who seemed to have a habit of bumping into everyone. Otis thought that if he walked like that in Alabama he'd soon be on the end of a serious Alabama ass wuppin'. (That was where someone gave you a thrashing to within an inch of your life, then picked you up and asked you, in all seriousness, 'Do you want some more?' People, if they could speak at all, usually declined the offer.)

He was amazed at the streets full of revellers, all in town because of the big show. He could hear some manic street preachers angrily railing against the High Street banks, God only knows why. Such serious people, and Welsh with it. There were crowds everywhere. It was clear that many came just to catch a glimpse of the famous stars in town for the big red-carpet event tomorrow.

Otis spotted a gaggle of the Leonard Co-hen party girls, all white heels and cleavages, evidently all into S&M (that is, you could divide them into a Suzanne or a Marianne. You could be one, but not the other). The Suzannes were being sisters of mercy, dispensing tea and oranges, which came all the way from the local Spar shop, to the unfortunate street people who had been moved into the side alleys. The Mariannes, much harder faced, just seemed to want to get away and say goodbye to all that.

At that moment sirens blared, and the police chief swept,

with a small army of officers, into the Boston Bakery and soon emerged, carrying large bags of white powder, cunningly labelled "flour". It looked like the chief's war on white powder was gathering pace. He'd soon be chief constable at this rate.

At the bridge near the river, Otis noticed a crowd of what looked like ancient holy men, with long wild hair and bare chests. *Ah*, smiled Otis, *the fanatical followers of James Jewel Osterberg Jr are in town!* As he got closer, he saw the clinching details: bare feet, no shirts, and shabby denim jeans. He'd been right – the Iggy Pop fan club had turned out in force. Their great guru must be close by.

For guys so old, he thought, *they've sure got a lot a lust for life, all right.*

Outside the Sugar Beet Club, he caught the end of an interview with Stalk 'n' Heads leader, David Byrne-Baby-Byrne. He was explaining that he had just ended his joint venture with Dior; he said that it was time to stop making scents, and to concentrate on the band's next album.

When Otis finally got up to his room, he switched on the local Brassica news channel to hear that Ozzy Osbourne had gone out on a pedalo into The Wash, looking for King John's crown jewels. It was Sharon's birthday on Sunday, and he wanted to give her something special. Latest reports were that he had been sighted just off Cromer, and was about to enter shipping lanes in the North Sea.

He flipped the channel to see Bob Gelded, the man who doesn't like Mondays, and the CEO of Banned Aid, the sticking plaster millionaire, pointing his finger and raving about the traffic.

Bob was saying, 'It's made worse by all these bands on the road, creating unnecessary pollution and congestion. The only bands that should be on the road are The Cars, the Drive-by Truckers, and that Van Morrison, the delivery guy. The rest should set an example and tour on cycles. Solo artists, like Bob Dylan, can go out on unicycles, and duos like Simon and Garfunkel, on tandems. We all have a duty, a duty to save the planet before it's too late, blah-blah-blah.'

He has a point, thought Otis, *but he's still a bit of a div.*

Just at that moment, Russ and Ron Mael of Sparks pedalled furiously past, waving to their adoring fans.

'Wow, always ahead of the game, those guys,' said Otis.

As their mudguards disappeared over the horizon, Otis noticed a strange glinting in the road ahead. As it approached, he was almost blinded by the sun bouncing off two magnificent pairs of spectacles. Who should it be but the tartan twosome, the Proclaimers, on their very own designer tartan tandem! They had a wicker basket on the front, and seemed to have a little mascot inside. It looked like a doll of Scotland's supremo, Nicola Sturgeon. As they passed by, Otis could see in fact that it actually was the wee lassie Nicola, in person! It never ceased to amaze him who turned up on these big occasions.

Before retiring for the night, Otis decided to walk down the riverbank to take the evening air. He noticed the river boys, Witham Willie Dixon, John Lee Humber and Nile Rogers, drifting by on a sugar beet party barge, probably chewing the fat about what was new on the waterfront that year.

Otis waved to Mike Scott and The Waterboys, who were strolling on the other bank, happy as sand boys. Otis wondered what that meant... Why were sand boys always happy? And more to the point, what exactly was a sand boy? Once again, he was stumped by the English language. But it was good to see Mike Scott's gang joking and smiling; they'd clearly got over their fisherman's blues.

He finally turned back towards the hotel, intending to get a good night's sleep, as tomorrow was shaping up to be a momentous day.

Just as he was reaching over to switch off the bedside lamp, he received a message from Daphne saying that he'd done really well that day at the rehearsal, especially since he wasn't, unlike all the other performers, used to being in the spotlight. Her message ended with: *Looking forward to seeing you tomorrow. Sleep well. Goodnight x.*

Otis, flushed with pride, sent back a shorter message simply saying: *Thanks. Good Luck tomorrow x.*

He thought long and hard before adding that final kiss, but in the end he sent it.

CHAPTER 25

The Big Day (and Night)

Otis woke up early. He'd been dozing, reviewing the time he'd spent in the UK, and in Lincolnshire in particular. It had been a wise decision to come there for the year. It had certainly helped him get over the painful divorce. She said that she never saw him, that he was married to his work and, on reflection, all that had been true. When she'd gone, life hadn't felt all that much different as they'd been living pretty much separate lives for some time. Still, it had been a bit of a shock when the final divorce papers had turned up at his address in Lincoln. He put those thoughts from his mind, as he began to focus on the big day ahead.

It was a media event like no other in Brassica; the awards show tonight was like the US NFL Superbowl, the Oscars and the All-Lincolnshire Open Conkers Championship all rolled into one. Everybody would be watching. That made Otis feel a little apprehensive, of course. He could feel the butterflies (probably cabbage whites) gathering in his stomach.

He knew that he was in for a long gruelling day so he chose oats for breakfast. (Oatmeal in the US, porridge or porage in the UK – such a complicated language.)

It was the nearest food he could get to the creamed grits of his childhood; in times of crisis, the ultimate Southern comfort food. His grandma back home used to call him "Oats" as a term of endearment, and he thought of her, and how she'd encouraged him to become the person he was today. If only she could have seen him at such a grand event like this, how proud she would have been.

This reminded him of a show he'd seen in Atlanta – a show by the great Alabama soul singer, Mr Clarence Carter, or Dr CC as he like to style himself. *Wouldn't have lasted long in academia*, thought Otis. *Only a soul singer could award himself a doctorate and get away with it.*

Clarence was famous for talking to his audiences; he often had long, rambling introductions to many of his famous songs. One time, he was talking about the past and how he missed the good ol' home cooking that his grandma used to make: fried chicken 'n' gravy, black-eyed peas, collard greens, candied yams.

Otis could see him, literally, licking his lips during the monologue and most of the audiences were too (no, not licking Clarence's lips, their own! Though knowing Clarence, he wouldn't have complained).

In the same show, Clarence had said that he'd had five wives and five divorces. Otis thought they'd never stayed around long enough to cook poor ol' Clarence a decent meal, that's why he was always hankering after his grandma's cooking...

It's strange how some childhood memories tend to stay with us, he thought.

Snapping out of this pensive mood, he turned on the local TV news and started to get ready. The big news was the arrival of Pope Bono the Great. The papal super yacht had sailed into Boston late last night and there were pictures of His U2ness blessing and laying hands on a couple of the Haven Hookers. He was reported to have "saved" quite a few of those girls over the years. He always seemed to enjoy his visits to preach in the big church, St Botolph's. He has often been heard to say that it was his favourite stumping ground.

Next up, a touching story – it was about one of those awards that Daphne had, unfortunately, had to cut from tonight's ceremony. To keep one of her major sponsors on board, Daphne had arranged for the award to be handed over and filmed for release, this morning, on breakfast television. Best Brassica Cosplay Costume had gone to Mrs Edna Duckering of Gedney Drove End, for her titanic iceberg lettuce costume. The citation from the judges, at The Co-operative Funeral Service, said her cos-tume was "seriously heavy, and hard-hearted. In fact, a real cabbage of a lettuce". Otis could see that it was, indeed, a worthy winner, though she was wilting a little under the studio lights. This was a reward "for persistence and resilience", said the judges. (Edna had entered the contest in, largely the same costume, for decades, but a few recent modifications had made all the difference.) She said that spending the night before the final in the sponsor's cold store had really helped to keep her edges crisp. Her determination and hard work had finally been recognised.

'Truly a standout performance,' agreed Otis. 'Indeed, a titanic iceberg that towered over the rest of the entries.'

The breakfast room in the hotel was even busier than yesterday. He could see Tom Hanks over by the cabbage juice bar talking to Joaquin Phoenix-Nights. Tom, Like Joaquin, had recently filmed scenes in Lincoln Cathedral. In Tom's movie *The Da Vinci Code*, Lincoln had stood in for London's Westminster Abbey, whereas in Joaquin's movie, it had been Notre Dame, Paris. *Lincolnshire folk sure were lucky, having such a talented cathedral that could turn its hand to such varied roles*, thought Otis.

He noticed far more food executives in the hotel that morning. At the next table to him, there was an animated conversation about potatoes and crisps, the kind of snacks the Americans confusingly called chips. Otis wondered, *why do these guys always seem to talk with their mouths full of food? Must go with the territory, I suppose.*

One guy was in favour of going hard into niche markets. 'Look how successfully our Quentin Crisps have penetrated the gay market and, once we'd put them in rainbow packaging, they went through the roof. We literally got the crisps packet and shook it up by the corner. Let's face it, guys, this is fast food, and some of these pedestrian brands can't keep up. Our new Sprinter range is going to be a winner, mark my words.'

Another crisp man said, 'It's true, there is traction in sporty names for snacks. I think we all remember a peanut bar called Marathon? I know, I know,' he said, 'the parent company changed its name to the US version – Snickers – but to be brutally honest, to a UK audience that has a flavour of underwear about it. Let's be fair, guys, left to our own devices we'd never call a snack "panties" or "g-strings"...'

A bright, young, and slightly deaf executive said, 'There is actually a snack called Cheese Strings.'

'You've got to be joking? What's that?'

'Erm, pieces of string, flavoured with cheese, I think...'

Someone else piped up. 'Actually that's one of our lines, and they're really rather good. The crispy, knotty bits are best.'

Otis, totally mesmerised by this exchange, decided it was time to leave. In the lobby he saw Gina Broccoli, fresh from the Cabbage event, where she'd helped launch the new Cabbage cell phone with the microwave oven, extendable trouser-press and underwater X-ray facility.

Otis wondered to himself whether it would still be possible to do something quaint and old-fashioned and actually make a telephone call on the thing.

Gina said, 'We must catch up, but I've a pressing meeting with our R&D boffins to put the finishing touches to our mega launch later today. Be sure to catch a monitor, and make sure to watch the ad breaks – we've a real blockbuster airing tonight!'

Over with the Cabbage executives, Otis noticed MC Hammer and Jimmy Nail, who were expected to perform a duet later. What could it all mean? There were also representatives from the Lincolnshire Fire Service and the NYFD. It was all very mysterious; the clouds of dry ice only adding to the atmosphere.

As he waited in line for coffee, he overheard another group of food executives – this time with Italian-American accents – talking pizza.

'What we have to do is encourage kids to play with their food. This will establish a bond that will stay for life. Who doesn't love their childhood toys?'

Where is this going? thought Otis.

'But parents are always telling kids *not* to play with their food.'

'Well, we have a radical new approach! Just listen to this, guys! We have this idea to make pizza in the shape of domino tiles. You know the game? It's a killer idea. The double-six is loaded with twelve dots of pepperoni, the double-blank is a veggie option. Six and a blank is half and half. It's gonna be massive. You can play with it then, of course, eat it. If you're losing, you can just distract your opponent and eat their pieces – game over! The idea is that you don't know which pieces will be in the packet, so we'll be encouraging kids to pester mums to bulk-buy to make a longer game of it. The party packs are going to be massive! Like I said, we have a winner on our hands here!'

Otis had a frightening vision of kids shoplifting pizzas to feed their new edible gaming addiction. Still, he had to admire the crazy logic of the whole thing.

As he went outside for some air, Otis noticed a definite tightening of security. He'd heard that the fabled Gedney Hill mountain rescue team had been engaged, though being the masters of disguise that they were, he hadn't seen them. Or, if he had, he hadn't noticed them. He'd spotted that they had a table reserved on Daphne's masterplan, but when he'd seen the tables at the rehearsal yesterday, theirs must have been the table with no name tags. *Bit of a giveaway, that*, he thought.

Otis went back up to his room to pick up his tuxedo before making his way back to the Starlight Rooms to get ready for the show.

The TV was still on, and a showbiz reporter was running through some earlier music media moments that had gone wrong.

She reminded us of the time Midge Ure had insulted the Austrian judges on Eurovision, when he'd said: "Ah Vienna, it means nothing to me." It was "nul points" for years after that. Midge never worked in Lederhosen again.

Perhaps the worst one was when John Lennon, while on The Beatles' tour of Yorkshire, told those people in Wensleydale that the Beatles were now bigger than cheeses. What an outcry that caused! People were melting down Beatles records and turning them into plant pots all over Yorkshire. Well, they couldn't just burn the damned things; after all, they'd shelled out hard-earned brass for them in the first place. This reminded Otis of similar things back home, when he was a kid in the Bible-belt.

He switched off the TV and went to the epicentre of the day's events. When he arrived there, Daphne was in a state of distress. Having had to rejig the running order yesterday, she was encountering more problems today. She'd been coming under huge pressure to reinstate the Barely Living Legend Award by its sponsors, the influential Billinghay Betamax Repairs and Spares Shop. They argued that it was a slight of almost satanic proportions to Keith Richards, as he'd won it for the last twenty-four years, and was hoping to get this year's special silver edition. Daphne stood firm.

She said, 'Look, he wasn't coming this year. He hasn't come for twenty-three of the last twenty-four years. I know, for a fact, that he's currently lying in a darkened room connected to a bank of Marshall amps in preparation for the Stones' grand centenary US tour later in the year.'

She was magnificent. Otis was impressed with her steely dismissal of those pygmies attempting to pressurise her. She did though give in to another pressure group. There was huge expectation in the county that after all their years of selfless service, Simply Dead would be honoured for playing at so many wakes, and for sending so many people on their way with such sweet music. An impressive group of supporters had been brought together overnight. The great and the good of Brassica really wanted this award to go ahead, and be recognised on live TV.

They won the day by getting local celeb Jonathan Van Tram to "sweet talk" Daphne into changing her mind. Jonathan, or JVT as he was more familiarly known, had risen to fame doing a series of teatime stand-up shows on national TV. Also, he was from Brassica, and he was a nice guy. He seemed a man you could trust. Daphne agreed on one condition: that JVT presented the award in person. He couldn't get out of that, but he had got the result he wanted (to use one of his famous football analogies).

Otis asked Daphne, a little later, what JVT had said to her that had made her change her mind.

She said, 'If I tell you, you must promise to keep it secret. This must go no further. I must insist on that. OK?'

Otis nodded and held his breath.

Daphne said, 'He told me that Simply Dead are one and the same group as Bruce's E-Stream Band. When not touring the world, they are back in Brassica, and to keep their hand in, they started playing at the wakes of famous local musicians – really to do something for their mates.'

So, thought Otis, *Jack Sabbath must have known this too. That's why he said they couldn't play at Bruce's wake. They'd obviously be far too upset...*

Daphne said, 'JVT's arranged for Woodhall Ska's Funeral Boy Three to play the gig instead.'

'My lips are sealed,' said Otis.

'Good boy,' said Daphne, patting him on the arm.

Otis glowed with pride, having been taken into her confidence.

Daphne said to Otis that after the show there would be photo opportunities on the red carpet for the paparazzi, and then several parties to attend.

'Several?' quizzed Otis.

'Yes,' said Daphne. 'It's very important to show your face, or these people think you've snubbed them.'

'We have Elton's bash – he has always loved returning to Bernie's home county – then the Brassica *Fair Magazine* party, and then the Cabbage Corporation do. Always spectacular food there. I've heard this year is a very good year for sprouts. And finally, a select few key players end up in Cultural Mick's for the best after-party ever. Stick with me, and make sure you wear this access-all-areas VVIP pass at all times. If we get separated, buzz me on my Cabbage watch.'

Daphne continued directing operations, and Otis went backstage and changed into his tuxedo. He put on his favourite western "bootlace tie"; *a nice American touch*, he thought. On the dressing table was the envelope he had to open later live in front of an audience of millions. He had to admit there were more than a few cabbage whites looping the loop in his stomach right now...

There was a loud knock, and Reg and Toby Carvery put their heads around the door. Otis was relieved to see familiar faces. They'd come to take him round some of the food industry tables, and to introduce him to some of the guests.

In this time before the show, guests were taking their seats, greeting old friends, and having drinks and canapés. Toby waved across to Nigella, who smiled back and raised her not inconsiderable eyebrows.

Across the room, Otis spotted a familiar face; a big star on cable TV in Alabama, Nigel "see ya later" Slater.

'He's the absolute darling of the trailer parks. His book, *Hampstead Roadkill*, was a big hit in the South,' Otis explained to Reg.

Toby said Nigel was the guy that had invented toast. He even wrote a book about it, adding, 'I think it was even made into a movie.'

Otis, who was clearly a huge fan, said, 'What made him a big star in Alabama was his simple mid-week skillet suppers, always with a twist. Folks seemed to like that in a chef. He's also so, so polite, no cuss words like some I could mention...' Otis was in his element now. 'Everyone was dazzled with his signature dish – the beans on toast – but Nigel's twist – to put the toast on top of the beans – was a masterstroke of sheer genius. I can still picture Nigel saying that eating it that way was a constant journey of discovery. I can still remember his very words: "Slicing into the toast, you get a tantalising glimpse of food Heaven... It's like an oyster full of twenty perfectly symmetrical orange pearls – utter bliss".'

Otis said Nigel had really earned a place in every Alabama cook's heart after his tip of spraying the pan, or the food, with

WD40, if you couldn't run to one of those fancy non-stick skillets.

Toby, who was also a fan and an acquaintance of Nigel's having worked on the *Brassica Cabbage Cookbook* with him, said, 'When Nigel feels like a fish-infused supper, he sometimes substitutes cod-liver oil capsules in place of the beans. He says the umami hit is incredible!'

'And, talking of mammy,' said Reg, 'there's Elena Wotsit-Carter, the unstoppable sex machine, who played Nigel's stepmum in the movie. What a star! Oh, and there's Johnny Dipp, too! All the big names are arriving now.'

Staff were weaving expertly between the crowds, carrying trays of food and drinks. Otis had never seen so much champagne being consumed.

Daphne stopped by and said, 'Robert de Niro's waiting.'

Otis was impressed. He'd heard that many actors took jobs waiting tables between more serious work. *What an example to younger actors*, he thought, before seeing that he was waiting to access the ultimate VIP lounge area.

That old trouper, Mavis Staples, had a job as a greeter, and if Otis heard her say, 'If you're ready, come, go with me,' once, he heard it a hundred times that night.

Otis noticed that many of the younger generation weren't actually eating their food; they were just photographing it.

Reg said that this was a real trend now, but in actual fact it had a long and noble history. He explained that when Brits first started going on holidays abroad, all the restaurants used to have photo menus so you could just point at your selection. It was fool-proof, especially for the Brits who were reluctant to accept that there were any other languages that made any sense apart from English.

Otis said, 'I suppose you could just take a photo of the photo, then cut out the bother of ordering and eating food that invariably went cold while searching for the correct filter to frame the perfect shot. Also, it would be great for those people who don't really like eating food but have social media accounts.'

'Exactly,' chimed Reg and Toby at the same time.

'Well, talk of the devil,' said Toby, 'there's the guy that started all this food and photography business.'

Otis looked around, but didn't see anyone he recognised.

'It's Helmit Newtown, the German photographer. His book, *The Naked Brunch*, is thought to have started this trend. Lots of bold black and white shots of really undressed salads, but ironically it's quite a saucy book!'

Reg chipped in, 'And a helluva big book, too. If you put legs on it, it'd easily make a decent sized coffee table.'

Otis, the cultural anthropologist, was loving this. Where else in his life had he had such a rich experience? Brassica, he was beginning to think, had changed his life. How was Alabama going to feel after this?

The show went remarkably well. Everyone was showering Daphne with praise. People were standing around exhausted, but getting themselves together for the gruelling round of parties.

'Some people have such a hard life,' joked Otis.

There was several dominant topics of conversation: Ozzie had reached Amsterdam, bought Sharon an old windmill, complete with a little mouse with clogs on, for her birthday. She was over the moon. She'd been trying to get him to record that song for years; the Cabbage ad was a great success and had been shared all over social media. *That's such a neat ruse*, thought Otis. *Only show the ad the one time, then let everyone else share it for you.* He remembered another great ad from a few years ago that had gone viral, as they said these days – that chocolate gorilla cookie ad where they'd trained Phil "Buster" Collins to play the drums! Nobody could believe it. Literally, billions of hits (not Phil, though he didn't have too bad a career) – the video.

The Cabbage ad starred Jimmy Nail from *Boyz from the Black Stuff*, the follow-up to Blaxploitation movie, *Boyz 'n the Hood*. Evidently the third in the sequence, based on Jimmy's early life in the ghetto in Stamford in the deep south of the county, is in production now at Cabbage Studios, its working title *Ghettover it!*

The ad was a big production number. Jimmy led a gang who turn on MC Hammer. The gang members all had their weapons of choice, the now fashionable personal flamethrower. They're a bit like the blowtorches that painters and decorators use, and those Glasgow gangs when they celebrated

Burns' Night. Hammer, wearing the new cabbage 'n' asbestos fire-retardant fabric suit, came on strong, singing *Can't Torch This*. The, for some reason, topless dancing firemen went down a storm, too. Cabbage had been inundated with orders from fire departments and defence contractors all over the planet. *What a result!* thought Otis, channelling JVT.

News was just in that the police chief had made his biggest haul yet. Operation White Powder had been renamed, as the chief thought it was a bit of a giveaway. Now it was called Operation WP after Wilson Pickett, it was alleged. There may have been some truth in that as the chief used to shout, 'One, two three! One, two, three!' then burst in, leading from the front. This latest haul comprised two gleaming stainless steel tanker trucks, chock full and cunningly labelled dried potato powder. Bit of a smash and grab raid, really. The news footage showed a lot of small alien types being led away in handcuffs. They could almost have been from the nearby *Star Wars* film lot. The chief was now grappling with the task of how to fit the trucks into the regulation-issue, tamper-proof evidence bags that everything had to be sealed in these days.

So much paperwork and red tape, it's a wonder they've any time at all to catch criminals, thought Otis. But Otis was pleased for him, thinking, *no one can really complain about the problems that success brings*. He was sure that the next time he bumped into the chief, he would be wearing the chief constable's uniform. *It's a good job they're about the same size*, thought Otis.

As they walked the few hundred yards to the marquee where Elton's bash was being held, Daphne suddenly grabbed Otis by the arm and said, 'Whatever you do, don't eat the canapés.'

Otis, who was feeling somewhat peckish after all the strenuous activity involved in opening that envelope, said, 'Why ever not? I thought that was part of the fun.'

Daphne said, 'There always a dodgy one. Last year, the "delicious" pistachio Turkish delights turned out to be Elton's grandpa's old suppositories. Evidently, a light dusting of icing sugar fools almost everyone, apart from those with the most discerning of palates.'

'No way! That's so gross!'

'And, what's more, some folks even asked for the recipe! He's a great practical joker, our Elton. He once told me – and this is strictly off the record – that he sends a box every year to Rod for his birthday. It's rumoured that he can't get enough of them by all accounts.'

The party always had a theme, and this year it was celebrating Brassica's Roman origins. The red carpet was lined with one hundred bronzed, oiled, and hunky centurions – fifty each side – who formed an arch by linking gold-plated sprout stalks. As they entered, there was Elton, resplendent in a leopard-skin Versace toga, saying a few words praising the three Caesar brothers: Jools, the warrior, who sent his legions to Brassica; Chicken Caesar, the cowardly one, a bit of a "wet lettuce" as they say in these parts; and Sid, who was a bit of a comedian.

Sid was the only one able to be present, and he stood up and took a round of drinks and applause. The others sent flowers – lilies, Elton's favourites. Elton said that the history books proved that Chicken Caesar, after inventing his salad, was the most name-checked Caesar of all time. Photos of him were all over social media; he was always on people's lips.

After Daphne had introduced Otis to several glamorous and exotic guests, he found himself being steered towards the host himself. Elton was deep in conversation with Anna Won-Ton, the editor of *Lincolnshire Vague*, the local style bible. Anna, looking immaculately cool as ever, turned to see Otis at the same moment as a waiter, bearing a tray of iced kale daiquiris, moved into the same space. Anna, Otis, and Elton formed a most indecorous heap on the floor. Otis, in his eagerness to help the others out, stood up to find himself holding two very different wigs. On the floor, two very bald people died a thousand deaths. Otis immediately fell down, releasing the hair-pieces, only to see that Anna now sported a fetching short brown back-combed hairdo, and Elton was completely hidden by a longer black number.

Daphne stepped in, smoothed Otis's tux and, to his great relief, they moved swiftly towards the exit. Otis did glance back once over his shoulder, and he still had nightmares about what he saw: a furious Elton pointing accusingly at Otis with one hand, and making a very definite thumbs down gesture with the other.

Local Roman expert, Professor Mick Jones who'd been employed as a consultant for the event, later told Otis that the atmosphere had turned even worse after one of his assistants had let slip, within Elton's earshot, that all the Roman roads were straight.

When they finally reached Cultural Mick's, the mood was much more relaxed. Daphne slipped off her stilettos and Otis loosened his tie as the place filled up with the usual suspects.

CHAPTER 26

The Happy Ever After Party?

Otis was somewhat relieved to hear that they'd just missed a set by local Goth sensations, Windows Made of Bricks. Admittedly, they'd done a tremendous one minute and fifty-nine-second version of Pink Floyd's *The Wall* but the rest was really very dark indeed. Daphne said that their stuff made Joy Division sound like the Wombles. Every time they got a radio play, sales of anti-depressants went through the roof.

Cultural Mick's was easily the fullest Otis had ever seen it. Mick had flown in from Brassnecker, his own luxury Caribbean retreat, and was proudly saying to all who would listen that they'd only be serving champagne from his own private vineyard this evening. Otis appreciated the dry, nutty flavour; a far cry from the stuff they drank from those Alabama wineries. As his eyes adjusted to the low-level lighting, he began to recognise people: Jack Sabbath who tipped his hat, Terry Vegetables, who seemed to be paying a little too much attention to Daphne; and Bob from Whittlesey, who was on his phone doing a deal to buy some more tropical fish from a dealer in Grimsby.

Was that really a good idea? wondered Otis. *Didn't Grimsby specialise in dead fish?*

Shane McGowan came over after fondly being reunited with his teeth framed behind the bar. He asked if anybody had seen the chief of police as he was hoping to do his annual singsong with the Brassica police choir.

'Not *Galway Bay* again?' said a ploughman, who'd been waiting for his lunch at the bar since... lunchtime.

Jack said to him, 'I think they've lost your order number, mate. This is a private party tonight. Just grab a Scotch egg.'

Reg Carvery came over and said the local van club were having their AGM in the backroom. This was, allegedly, a very exclusive club with considerable sway in the Brassica region; a bit like a cross between a secret society and a powerful trade union. All the major van drivers were there: Don O'Van, Vangelis, Van Halen and, of course, Van the Man, the Morrison's delivery man. Local luminary, Jonathan Van Tam (now of course since moving to Nottingham, Van Tram) was the group's honorary president.

Toby joined them, saying he'd just been party to a fascinating conversation between local Brassica luvvies his lordness Andrew Loud Webbed-Feet (as his name suggests, from one of the oldest Fenland families), and his words-man, Sir Tom Rice, of the Fenland paddy field dynasty. They'd had a word with Van the Man and wanted to do a stage show/musical/biopic. They'd quickly run through his CV and they were certain that there was enough to hold an audience in thrall, in fact enough to hold an audience anywhere.'

And in truth, thought Otis, *it was a remarkable career trajectory.* He'd started off as one of Them in Belfast, living next door to Kenny "Oscar" Branner. He then gave Them the slip and went to California; got a bad dose of the hippies; recorded that protest album attacking Big Oil, Castrol Reeks, only to finally end up here in Brassica, driving a van, delivering veg for the family firm of Morrison's.

'He can be a bit of a grumpy old bugger sometimes, from what I've read in *KO Magazine*,' said Daphne.

'That's because he doesn't suffer fools, and why should he?' said Otis. 'By all accounts, he's a bit of a perfectionist.'

'Well, he'd be just perfect for their show.'

This brought to mind a Webbed-Feet-Rice number he'd heard an urchin singing in one of the back streets of Spilsby: *Georgie Best Superstar, wears frilly knickers, and he wears a bra!*

Great stuff, thought Otis, wondering, who this Georgie Best fellow was. *If only there was a Belfast connection, now that would be perfect...*

Word was that the police chief had hot-footed it over to Bardney on learning that there was a sugar beet factory hiding in full view. Latest reports suggested that he was asking RAF Coningsby if they could store two and a half tons of white powder, cunningly labelled "sugar", in one of their largest hangars. *That guy's incredible, he works so hard*, thought Otis.

Now there's a guy whose life would make a great bio-pic. But would they be able to lure such a dedicated public servant like police chief Rob Lowe all the way across the pond to Hollywood? Otis rather doubted it.

The chief was supposed to be there. He always attended the after-party, even if largely to keep an eye on ace rapper Gangmaster Flash and his posse of William McGonagall wannabees. Daphne assured Otis that the chief would be there at some point. When she'd been to the ladies' she'd noticed the door to the snug was open, and all those young Brat Pack guys were there again.

Otis said, 'Remember that movie, *The Outsiders*? Had all those guys in it. Tom Waits too, now I remember. Great theme music as well, *Gloria* by a band called Them. Maybe you ought to take Van the Man in to meet them – that'd be really cool.'

Daphne said that she didn't know him that well, and he could be awkward. 'Maybe another time...' which Otis took to be no!

Otis, who had really begun to relax now, wandered over to Shane McGowan at the bar and, plucking up courage, said, 'Excuse me, Mr McGowan, but I've always wondered what exactly a pogue is. Would you be so kind as to enlighten me?'

Shane, quickly taking in Otis's access-all-areas VVIP pass, said, 'Well, Professor Otis K Spanner III, this is what a pogue is.' And he planted a huge wet smacker of a kiss on Otis's left cheek. 'A pogue is an old Irish word for a kiss, a smackeroo, a snog.'

Slightly flustered, Otis thanked him and went back to his seat.

'I see you're getting acquainted with the stars,' teased Daphne, and she boldly planted a kiss on Otis's other cheek!

Otis's blood pressure surged.

At that moment, Terry Hall, the man who put the Hall in Woodhall Ska, came in with the rest of Funeral Boy Three, half of Bananarama, and some other guys Otis didn't recognise.

Jack Sabbath wandered over and said to Otis, 'It's on for tonight!'

'What is?' said Otis.

'The Boss's send-off.'

'Tonight? It's almost tomorrow now!'

'Well, the early hours. It's best under the cover of darkness,' Jack said. 'It's all his own wishes. He didn't want the usual wailing in the streets, but didn't want a Gram Parsnips-style cock-up, either. There's rock and roll and there's rock and roll, if you know what I mean.'

Otis wasn't too sure he did, but he did remember the trouble when Gram had died in The Joshua Tree Hotel in California back in '73. His road manager and an old Byrds' roadie kidnapped his body from LAX and drove it back to Cap Rock in the Joshua Tree National Park, and decided, in line with something Gram (probably while under the influence of mescal or mushrooms) had said, to cremate him and scatter his ashes there. Unfortunately, for them, some tourists saw this somewhat unusual BBQ and called the cops. Gram's family in

New Orleans weren't too pleased when they heard the news. The judge made the two roadies pay for the funeral in Louisiana. So there is some justice in the world, after all...

Jack said, 'A boat, a special one, has been sourced and delivered, thanks to those Gedney Hill mountain rescue boys, and it's going to be towed for Bruce's last journey down the river into The Wash. It's the Viking hero's funeral that he deserves. The boat and the body will be burnt, and will dissolve and scatter across the water and into the ocean and the air.'

Otis felt a lump rising in his throat and tears in his eyes.

Otis had only been to one rock 'n' roll funeral, but for Alabama that had been a big one. When Lynyrd Skynyrd's plane went down, he ended up going, as a young man, to Johnny Van Zant's send-off in Florida. He thought it was real neat that Neil Young had been one of the coffin bearers. It showed that Neil knew that not all southern men were bad. Neil and Ronnie had been good friends. Neil even wrote a song – *Powderfinger* – for the band.

This serious mood was interrupted with a loud announcement – it was Lettery time!

This had started years ago as a means of shaking up the music scene. With all the music executives in town, this had become a great way of combining business with a lot of fun. Some interesting new combos had emerged. It worked a bit like the FA Cup draw, but with three participants. Bands who were feeling a little tired, or felt they needed a blood transfusion of talent, could enter the competition. Only certain bands were eligible – strict house rules – bands with names made up of letters: REM, ELO, NWA, ABC, KLF, XTC, OMD, AC/DC, and, occasionally, numbers were allowed, like MC5 or UB40. All the letters were put into a bag and Terry Vegetables, Damon All-Bran and Nana Moussaka would draw balls out, creating new bands. Only ever had two mishaps when they'd created the PLO and WD40. Some groups did well, even as leftovers. That's how Booker T found his MGs, and how the BGs were born. It could get a bit messy towards the end, with agents and managers always falling out. The utter dregs were never wasted, and they've made some great radio stations for the foreign market. Radio KYJ became very popular Down Under.

Toby Carvery introduced Otis to the great Japanese designer, Feng Shui, who had a black belt in moving furniture about. He was very much in demand, and had saved the Cabbage Corporation millions by slightly re-aligning several hundred square miles of glasshouses to catch a couple more minutes of precious sunshine each day.

Otis told Daphne about the plans for the Boss's send off. She said that he would be sorely missed.

'None of that highly varnished "Fancy Dan" yacht rock nonsense here,' she said. 'Bruce was proud of being a hard-working man and he'd virtually created the genre of "barge rock" single handed. Never left the area. Hell, he even married a dredger's daughter. They worked tirelessly to keep Brassica moving with the times.' She suddenly looked tired, and said, 'Let's go back to the hotel, I'm totally done in. It's been one of the longest days of my life.'

As they were getting ready to move, the doors burst open and the chief of police entered to a round of applause. He was wearing an orange hi-vis jacket that had the word *salt* written in large luminous letters. On the way back from the successful "sugar" raid in Bardney, they'd noticed a council depot full of heavy trucks and mounds of grit and salt, ready for the winter roads. Not content with waging a war on white powder, he'd now turned his attention to those large mountains of crystals.

Otis noticed that one of the officers, not unlike the man he'd seen leaving the Daily Sex Institute, was wearing a hi-vis jacket with the word *twat* on his back. He asked Jack what that was all about, and Jack had said that all depots had one of those in case the prime minister turned up. He was in the habit of appearing on the TV news most nights wearing that kind of thing.

Otis said, 'Isn't that a bit disrespectful?'

Jack said, 'He never notices, it's on his back. All he does is look at the cameras, smile, stick one or two thumbs up, then he buggers off.'

Daphne and Otis linked arms and walked briskly, in the moonlight, towards the Five Seasons, the only building in the town higher than the famous Stump. As they reached the lift, Daphne kissed him. She thanked him for all his support over the last few days. She said to come up to her room as she had the penthouse suite, and the best panoramic views in town.

They stood by the window looking down on the damp

flatlands of the Fens, where the roads and dykes were straight, and the only bent things were the hooks on the eel fishermen's lines. A heady aroma of cabbage and sprouts pervaded the evening air.

'Ah, sweet home, Brassica!' murmured Daphne.

They could just make out the burning vessel moving slowly out to the open mouth of the mighty Wash. A crescent moon cast a thin coating of silver on the slow-moving waters of this fecund earthly paradise. The strains of Floyd's *Wash You Were Here* could just be heard wafting in on the breeze.

Daphne said, 'I love this version by the Austrian Pink Floyd, the one with the yodelling and the great alpenhorn solo.'

Otis said he preferred the original, but they weren't going to fall out over it. He looked across at Daphne and wondered, *could I be happy here? Maybe I should give it a try...*

They stayed there on the roof until the boat had finally disappeared and the first streaks of daylight spread across the sky.

'The Boss is dead, long live the Boss! The music will live for ever!'

Later, much later, Otis woke up feeling wistful. In fact, he'd never felt this full of wist in his whole life.

CHAPTER 27

After the Lord Mayor's Show... Back to Reality

So, what happens next? wondered Otis as he drove back from the somewhat temporary bright lights of Boston to Lincoln. Clearly there was much thinking to be done. The last few days had felt like he was inhabiting one of those rather tacky souvenir snow globes and some huge, unknown force had been picking it up and shaking it every few hours.

Back at his desk in his university office he was confronted with a tsunami of emails, voicemails and a schedule of meetings that made his mood slump. It felt like he was still trapped in that snow globe and someone had just given it a particularly violent shake.

Oh well, you've got to take the rough with the smooth, he thought.

At that moment the phone rang and the Head of School's PA asked if he could come to a meeting at two p.m. that afternoon. Otis had been planning to review the current status of his research before considering what to do next. He asked about the agenda for the meeting and was met with vague statements about how the Head of School hadn't seen him for quite a while and that it would be good to "touch base", whatever that meant. The words "staffing" and "hours" were also mentioned.

Uh oh, here we go again... thought Otis.

He suggested meeting the next day, Friday, but then remembered that trying to get hold of a senior academic on a Friday was almost impossible. "Research days" had a habit of making the usual two-day weekend into something far more palatable. Otis had quickly learned that the only poor saps teaching on Fridays were part-timers, or those whose stock was particularly low. Who knows what heinous crimes those timetabled to teach on a Friday afternoon had committed?

So, a meeting later in the day it was.

After binning the vast majority of his emails, he felt a little more in control of events. Now it was time to start pulling things together. What had he achieved so far? Had Lincolnshire lived up to his expectations? How did it compare to his home state of Alabama? He wondered if, for example, he had been comparing Northamptonshire and Nebraska, would he have come up with similar findings.

Lincolnshire indeed, like Alabama, was not very well-known in its own country. In the course of his research, Otis had come across a comment by the journalist and author, Matthew Engel, that Lincolnshire was "intriguing, distinctive, full of the unexpected". He also said that the place really suffered from "low self-esteem" and, in truth, Otis couldn't disagree with most of that – he had come to pretty much the same conclusions himself. It was true that the place had thrown up some remarkably unexpected musical surprises.

Otis felt that Lincolnshire had some of the "independent otherness", a kind of "island" feel to it. Perhaps not surprising since The Humber bordered its old northern edge, the North Sea skirted its eastern coast, and The Wash and the Fens wetted its southern extremities. Just to finish things off, the River Trent trickled down its inside leg or, somewhat more paradoxically, flowed up it.

Both Lincolnshire and Alabama were largely rural areas and people tended to fall back on stereotypes when describing them. Otis knew there was nothing inherently wrong with stereotypes – they were based on real perceptions – but on their own, they only gave a partial snapshot of the bigger picture. So, Lincolnshire was always "flat" but Otis had found that that was only partly true and then, especially, in the southern Fenland parts of the county. Equally, there was a type of American who tended to look down with pity on Alabama as a poor, backwards kind of place. Indeed, the kind of place that you would never recommend to friends planning to visit the United States.

On his travels, Otis had seen the monument erected to the Pilgrim Fathers at Fishtoft, just outside Boston – a simple, small granite obelisk. What was strange about the monument was that it commemorated a place that they in fact didn't sail from. The citation stated that they were "thwarted in their attempt to sail to find religious freedom across the sea". Somehow that seemed so typically Lincolnshire – a monument erected to celebrate where something didn't happen!

In his extensive travels around this very large English county, Otis had recorded its musical heritage and its contribution to modern popular culture. Who could have predicted the strong Michael Jackson links? Or the phenomenal coincidence that connected songwriters Bernie Taupin and Rod Temperton to a small, unprepossessing market town on the edge of the Lincolnshire Wolds? Not forgetting the distinctive and varied contributions of Gainsborough, Grimsby, Lincoln, Louth, Stamford and Woodhall.

At first, it had seemed to Otis that Lincolnshire's musical heritage was much more eclectic than that of Alabama's where, to all intents and purposes, country music reigned supreme... But then again, there was southern rock and boogie; not forgetting the soul and funk output from the Muscle Shoals studios. Otis noted that country music was largely the preference of local white folks, while the soul and funk artists who recorded in the Shoals tended to be black (except of course Eddie Hinton who was white, but sounded as if he were Otis Redding's twin brother). What surprised all those great soul singers was the fact that all the studio session musicians – the Muscle Shoals rhythm section – had all been local white guys.

Otis had certainly not known what to expect when he came

over to Lincolnshire. It really was a world away from what he had been used to in the South... And yet both areas were off the beaten track and largely left to their own devices. Maybe his work, when finally published, would encourage more people to come and explore the musical heritage of Lincolnshire and the Brassica region.

It was almost two p.m. and time for his meeting with the Head of School. He gathered his notes and his laptop and went up to her office. She greeted him warmly and said how pleased the university was that he had made a contribution to the prestigious Brassica FM Music and Food Awards. She added that the vice chancellor had also recognised his participation in this important local event. Otis had noticed in his year here how fast the university authorities moved to boost any scintilla of positive news, invariably issuing self-congratulatory press releases, showing how central and important it was to the local economy.

As the Head of School's voice droned on, Otis found his gaze wandering to the view outside the window. He had to agree that the university could only be seen as a force for good in the county. He had heard that before being established on this city centre brownfield site, some had argued for it to be located on the edge of town, on the site of a redundant Victorian lunatic asylum. Otis thought that without the university at the heart of the city, Lincoln would have been like a donut with a huge hole in the middle...

After enquiring about the progress of his research, the

Head of School told him that she would need to "re-deploy" one of his research assistants, as a junior member of staff had met with an unfortunate accident and she needed urgently to cover his undergraduate teaching commitments. There was nothing really Otis could do, and he thought why make a fuss when most of the field trips had now been completed. (Incidentally, he later found out on the university grapevine that the "unfortunate accident" had involved the young lecturer who had been in line at the local food bank when a volunteer had inadvertently dropped a case of Tesco value baked beans onto his foot, causing several painful and complicated metatarsal fractures.)

After further general chatting about how quickly the year had flown, Otis left the meeting and returned to his office.

Otis switched on the radio to catch the last few minutes of Daphne's afternoon show. People had been showering her with praise for the way she had presented the Music and Food Awards show. He could tell from her voice that she was both happy and exhausted.

They had arranged to meet after work to go for something to eat. *A proper meal, after last night's carnival of canapés, would go down very well*, he thought. Daphne said she would choose the place, which was a big relief to Otis as he would have struggled to find somewhere suitable.

He picked her up at seven p.m. that evening, and she said that she'd booked a table at a pub, The Dambusters Inn, a country pub in Scampton, a village a few miles outside Lincoln.

The stone-built village pub was what Otis thought a typical English pub should look like. Well, perhaps not quite typical; it was a veritable shrine to the Dambusters 617 Squadron, which had been based at RAF Scampton air station during the Second World War. The pub was chock-full of wartime memorabilia: medals, photographs, even aeroplane tyres from Lancaster bombers. In fact, almost everything except, thankfully, bombs.

The pub was also a micro-brewery and the landlord gave Otis a crash course in what constituted real ale. As Otis was the designated driver he wasn't drinking that night, otherwise it might have literally been a crash course. However, he'd soon heard more than enough to be already planning another return visit soon.

On the way back to town, Daphne noticed a CD case sticking out from underneath the passenger seat and, with a rather gymnastic contortion, she retrieved it to find that it was empty but that the cover was a list of handwritten tracks that Otis had put together; a kind of CD equivalent of a mixtape. She asked Otis what it was and he said it was a compilation of some of his favourite tracks from back home in Alabama. He said he preferred the handpicked, handmade artefact, rather than just Bluetooth music linked to some random speaker. He said that he had made it to play on the long drives around the county to remind him of home. However, he'd only ever listened to it on his own, and since he'd discovered Radio Brassica, he said he hadn't listened to it for months.

Daphne looked at the handwritten list of tracks. There were songs and artists that she recognised, like Dr CC, Lynyrd Skynyrd, and Alabama Shakes, but lots that she had never come across, like Eddie Hinton, Jason Isbell, Arthur Alexander, and the Drive-By Truckers.

'Where is this CD?' she asked Otis. 'Can we play it?'

'If it's not in the case, it's probably in the player.'

'May I?' said Daphne, as she reached over and pressed play. Track one, DBT...

What happened next changed her life for ever; a five-minute thirty-eight-second aural assault. If it hadn't been for her seatbelt she might well have been blown back to Scampton, but the speakers in the back of the car seemed to be forcing them forwards, creating a vortex of white-knuckle sound. When it had finished, the silence enveloped them.

'*What* on earth was that?' she asked.

'*Marry Me*,' he said.

She turned to Otis, confused.

'The best song I've ever seen them play live – *Marry Me*. Definitely one of my all-time favourites.' Otis reached forward and turned off the player. He turned again to look at Daphne and simply said, once more, 'Marry me.'

She looked him in the eyes, smiled and, nodding her head, said, 'I think that's a very good idea... And by the way, that's a yes!'

APPENDICES

CHAPTER 1
* *Buttholeville Bugle*: Buttholeville, the archetypal Southern Anywheresville, taken from a 1999 Drive-By Truckers' song.

CHAPTER 2
* *Burning Love* was originally recorded by Arthur Alexander, but it was written by Dennis Linde. Arthur wrote the other songs mentioned in the chapter.

CHAPTER 3
* River cruise ships could sail to Gainsborough, but sadly none ever did. Well, not yet...
* Robert Stigwood did manage the Bee Gees and many other acts. It's not known if he ever scouted for bands in Gainsborough, but who knows, he might well have done.

* The Poole brothers really do exist and Darren/Ben has successfully directed and starred in a number of large-scale community plays in Lincoln Cathedral. He played the lead role in *Jesus Christ Superstar* to great local acclaim.
* The family did open a teashop – *Imperial Teas* – on Lincoln's aptly named Steep Hill.
* Alexis and Caenby Korner: Alexis Korner was an influential British blues musician in the late 1950s and 1960s; Caenby Corner is a roundabout on the A15, between Gainsborough and Market Rasen.
* Mr English really was the name of the reference librarian in Gainsborough. I have this information on the good authority of Dr Ian Waites, an ex-colleague, who frequently visited the library as a child.
* "Scunny" is a local, familiar term for Scunthorpe.
* Uncle Wilbur's ghost suit refers to his Klansman's robes.
* "R White" is the name of a manufacturer of a popular brand of lemonade in the UK.
* Etherwood-Edward "Woody" Allen is a record producer and singer-songwriter on the *Med School* and *Hospital Records* labels. The genre is drum and bass, but essentially it's just great music. He grew up near Stow and his family still live in the area.

CHAPTER 4

* King Edwards, Charlotte, Nicola, Maris Piper and Desiree are all varieties of potatoes.

* The Walker Gallery is in Liverpool, not Walkers, which is a brand of UK potato crisps.
* Eccles is in Manchester, England.

CHAPTER 5
* Sydney Malkinson & Gliderdrome details were taken from www.thegliderdrome.com.
* *Meet on the Ledge* is a Richard Thompson song for Fairport Convention.
* Rob Lowe, a US actor, appeared in a 2019 TV series *Wild Bill* (six episodes), where he played a police chief who moves from Miami to be Police Chief Constable Bill Hixon in Boston, Lincs. The show was cancelled after series one.
* Oliver Double is a former stalwart of the Yarborough School, Lincoln Drama Department. He became a stand-up comedian and an academic at the University of Kent. He is the author of several serious books on comedy.
* It is believed that, in the absence of the real *Pink Floyd*, there is a successful *Australian Pink Floyd* act.
* Irishman Arthur Ryan did start a company called Primark, though if he did pioneer clothing made from potatoes, he kept it very quiet. He did miss a trick not using RyanWear as a brand name.
* For some reason, there really is a Scottish lifeboat stranded outside Baytree Garden Centre, near Spalding.
* Jimi Hendrix' UK double album *Electric Ladyland* featured a bevy of naked women on its cover. The US version didn't.

CHAPTER 6
* "The Vinyl Triangle" is so called because of three record stores visited by some collectors on the South Lincs/Cambs border. Uptown Vinyl near Spalding, Bob's Records in Whittlesey, and a smaller shop above a barbershop in Market Deeping (now closed).
* Baytree Garden Centre is an extraordinary place – much more than a mere garden centre.
* "Cubby" Broccoli really did produce a number of the earlier James Bond films.

CHAPTER 8
* Long John Baldry was the singer's real name – not Baldy.

CHAPTER 9
* There is a BFI National Archive film available on YouTube of Bardney Pop Festival, 1972.
* "Yellowbelly" is a term referring to people and things from Lincolnshire.

CHAPTER 11
* Terry Vegetables refers to Terry Venables, former footballer & England manager.
* Gibraltar Point is on the east coast of England, south of Skegness, towards The Wash.

CHAPTER 12

* The council in Grimsby really did have a campaign using high-pressure water hoses to leave messages about litter and graffiti in the grime on the streets... bizarre.

CHAPTER 13

* Dave Formula, aka Dave Tomlinson, was in the post-punk band Magazine (and in Visage). Their third album was called *The Correct Use of Soap*. Only they know why.
* Crackpots was an "arty-crafty" café on Queen Street, Louth, run by talented potter and sculptor Elaine. She really did have a bust of Robert Wyatt explode. Sadly, the café closed in 2022.
* Robert Whynot refers to Robert Wyatt, drummer and vocalist of Soft Machine and creator of many fine solo albums. He settled in Louth with his wife, artist Alfreda Benge, and has lived there for many years. She designed the covers for his solo albums.
* "Larders and jammy jars" are words taken from some of Wyatt's extraordinary lyrics.
* Graham Fellows is an actor and comedian. He tours as the musician John Shuttleworth. His 1978 single, *Jilted* John, was championed by Radio 1 DJ John Peel, and it reached number four in the UK charts.

CHAPTER 14
* Canwick-on-Witham, or Washingborough, has always been called Washingborough.

CHAPTER 15
* Billy Pritchard is originally the name of a character and song by the great Brent Best for his band Slobberbone (New West Records 2002).
* Mick Jones is an archaeologist and Roman expert who headed up the Lincoln Archaeology Unit for many years.
* UTC refers to "Up The Chimps" – what fans post on social media sites.
* "Barefoot Nights" refers to Barefoot, a popular Lincoln collective of mainly soul music fanatics. They hold regular, very successful vinyl nights in venues ranging from cosy pubs to Lincoln Castle.

CHAPTER 17
* Ketwood is actually called The Petwood Hotel.
* "Rude boys and girls" is a term originating from Jamaican street culture, now more generally applied to fans of two-tone/ska music.
* "Pork-pie hat" is so called because of its shape and not, alas, for what it is made of.

CHAPTER 19
* Rob Lowe appeared in the film version of SE Hinton's novel *The Outsiders*, together with all the other actors mentioned in the chapter.

CHAPTER 20
* Lane cake is the official state cake of Alabama. It is mentioned in Harper Lee's *To Kill a Mockingbird*.

CHAPTER 24
* Jim Broadbent is an Oscar-winning actor who grew up in Lincolnshire. Early in his career he performed in the two-man comedy theatre troupe The National Theatre of Brent, alongside Patrick Barlow.

CHAPTER 25
* It is, in fact, not a good idea to eat, ingest or swallow WD40, as it is derived from petroleum distillates. Not recommended orally, or aurally.
* Helmit Newtown refers to Helmut Newton, the fashion photographer.

CHAPTER 27
* Matthew Engel quotes are taken from *Engel's England*, Profile Books (2014).
* The Dambusters Inn is in Scampton village, serving good food and locally brewed beer.

* *Marry Me* is a song on the *Decoration Day* album (2003) by the Drive-By Truckers.

ACKNOWLEDGEMENTS

Many thanks to Kirsty Jackson, Victoria Richards, Shannon Chapman and the rest of the Cranthorpe Millner team. Also, I'd like to thank the following for their support and encouragement over the years: my children Cait and James, Professor Amanda Roberts, and Peter Roe and Ian Waites, the latter two being long-time members of our regular Friday evening sessions in The Strugglers Inn, Lincoln. I also pay tribute to fellow drinkers, Ric Metcalfe, Mick Jones, Grahame Lloyd, Pat Sikorski, Darrell Hair and Amanda Spalding . Cheers !

ABOUT THE AUTHOR

Mike Murphy has lived in Lincoln for half a century. He worked in secondary schools and latterly in the School of Design at the University of Lincoln. He also spent half a semester in a high school in South Carolina. Before all that, he lived in another fine cathedral city, York, though like John Ruskin, he thinks that Lincoln is the finest of all English cathedrals. When not listening to his extensive vinyl music collection, Mike can be found reading the works of Christopher Brookmyre, Jonathan Coe, Carl Hiaasen, Elmore Leonard, David Lodge, Spike Milligan and David Nobbs. He also plays tennis (sort of...)and tends his allotment garden.